L'IMMORTALITÉ

MADAME LALAURIE
AND THE VOODOO QUEEN

L'IMMORTALITÉ

MADAME LALAURIE
AND THE VOODOO QUEEN

T. R. HEINAN

Nonius LLC

Published by Nonius LLC
7739 E. Broadway Blvd.
Suite 54
Tucson, AZ 85710

First Edition

Manufactured in the United States

EAN-13: 978-0615634715

ISBN-10: 0615634710
Library of Congress Cataloging in publication data

Library of Congress Control Number: 2012938728
CreateSpace, North Charleston, SC

TABLE OF CONTENTS

Acknowledgements

The author would like to thank BCD for suggesting and assisting with this project; Rachael for her special assistance; and Pat, Tim, Molly, and Bigfoot Joe for all their help and for putting up with two years of my chatter about Delphine Lalaurie.

Thanks also to Scott and Jeff for their technical support and to the professional tour guides in New Orleans who keep this haunting legend alive night after night.

Front cover and illustrations by

John Weston
Los Angeles, CA

A Note on Historical Context

While this story is intended to entertain, I have also tried to convey the harsh realities of life in early nineteenth-century New Orleans. For this reason, this book employs certain terms that, fortunately, have become outdated. One cannot do justice to describing the period without taking notice of a complex and unique social structure that was based on race, color, and national origin. Many of these distinctions often relied on fictional accounts of bloodlines and were, of course, rooted in prejudice. Marie Laveau, a free woman of color, would have objected to being called black. It was a time when "colored" meant having some European ancestry, while "black" meant "slave" and being, or at least appearing, entirely African. Marie called herself "Creole." The French community had an entirely different understanding of "Creole," and most even objected to the term "American."

It is also difficult to overstate the influence Catholicism had in antebellum New Orleans. Louisiana's history as Spanish and then French territory meant that the Catholic Church played an enormous role in giving the city a flavor that was very different than other parts of the South. The infamous Code Noir did little to soften the appalling injustice of slavery, yet it did play a part in exposing the horrible treatment of slaves. New Orleans's unique gumbo of religious and racial history made it possible for the body of Marie Laveau to be placed in the same cemetery as her white neighbors, but prevented her from attending their schools.

It is still possible to visit many of the historic New Orleans sites that form the backdrop for this story. Touring the French Quarter can be a delightful way to learn about the resilience and national influence of this great city. I urge readers to visit Saint Louis Cathedral, Pirates Alley, the Cabildo, Congo Square, and even, late at night, the truly haunted Lalaurie mansion.

—**T.R. Heinan**

Prologue

New Orleans was coming alive. The bells of Saint Louis Cathedral chimed seven o'clock. At Saint Louis Cemetery No. 1, the gates had closed to visitors four hours ago, but the old sexton voiced no objection to the woman creeping past the grave of Homer Plessy. He'd seen her before.

She slipped between the white parapet tombs and oven vaults of the burial ground, pausing for a moment by a stepped chamber engraved with the name Philippe Bertrand.

A red-and-white scarf shrouded her face. She paused, allowing the coral pink shades of twilight to silhouette her slender frame before she passed between the graveyard's whitewashed gateposts. She was leaving this cemetery for the last time, she hoped. The sexton smiled as he closed the squeaky black iron gate behind her.

Once on Basin Street, the woman set down the lidded basket she was carrying and adjusted the belt on her long grey coat. Her mission now was to find and help a certain young man who made his living as a tour guide. At this hour, she was sure she knew where he'd be.

Over on Bourbon Street, Carl and his wife were relishing the street performers and sipping slushy hurricane drinks from plastic go-cups.

"Betcha a dollar I can tell you where you got them shoes."

Carl ignored the hustler. He'd already fallen for that line once. He was far more interested in the scantily clad young woman who was trying to entice him into a strip club.

Carl's wife tugged at his arm, causing him to spill a few drops of his red frozen drink on a T-shirt emblazoned with the words "I" and "Duluth," a red Valentine heart placed between the two words. The heart matched Carl's red Bermuda shorts.

"Come on, Carl, we're going to be late for the haunted tour."

Music blared from one of the nearby clubs, trumpet, sax, bass, and drums playing somebody's request for "When the Saints." The band charged extra for that song. Carl's wife began to sing along, "I want to be in that number..."

The couple veered right off Bourbon Street. Ten minutes later, they were standing on Governor Nicholls Street, formerly known as Hospital Street. With them were four other tourists, each wearing little white tags to identify them as paid members of the haunted tour group. At their rear stood the woman who had walked out of Saint Louis Cemetery, her face still hidden by her scarf. She'd found the tour guide and studied him as she leaned against the gray shuttered window of a faded pink house. Carl and his wife stood in front of her.

The young tour guide kept a black umbrella in his left hand and clutched a small blue object in his right. He used the umbrella to point to the rectangular gray stucco house on the corner across the street. Tall, arched windows surrounded its first and third floors. Rectangular windows with black shutters looked out from behind the wrought-iron gallery on the second floor.

The tour guide fidgeted with the license dangling from his belt and did his best to conceal the blue object in his right hand. Carl's wife took a disposable flash camera out of her purse and, without looking, stepped back. Her beehive hairdo bumped the shrouded face of the woman from the cemetery.

"Sorry."

The mysterious woman didn't look up or respond.

The tour guide stepped off the curb, into the street.

"We've arrived at 1140 Royal Street, what many believe to be the most haunted house in New Orleans. In 1833, this house belonged to Madame Delphine Lalaurie and her husband. The ineptitude of these two villains might have been comedic but for its tragic toll in human life."

The guide paused to prevent his story from being obscured by the clopping hooves of a passing mule-drawn carriage.

"In truth," he continued once the carriage had passed, "the suffering they caused behind those walls was so horrible, so horrific, that it pierced the fabric of immortality and still haunts this house today."

The slurping of a take-away hurricane through a plastic straw prompted the tour guide to pause once again. Carl's wife poked him with her elbow, causing him to spill the remainder of the bright red mixture of juice, rum, and grenadine onto the sidewalk.

The mysterious woman could no longer hear Carl's slurping, the tour guide's voice, or the passing traffic. Her attention was focused on the thick red liquid from Carl's cup as it poured out onto the street.

Chapter 1

Madame Lalaurie's Wish

JUNE 1833

Dim morning light bestowed a dark burgundy hue to the slave's blood as it poured onto the broad cypress slats of the attic floor. Muffled moans and a harmonica playing in the background masked the buzzing of flies circling above rusty buckets filled with body parts.

Inches above the floor, a thin stream of sunlight projected through small, half-opened shutters, painting a bright rectangle of radiance in front of the slave's shackled feet. It provided just enough light to reveal Dr. Louis Lalaurie's bloody apron and even bloodier cleaver.

Forty-eight-year-old Louis Lalaurie was a soft, pudgy, balding man whose chubby pink hands were now smeared with blood.

He kept his sleeves rolled up to his elbows, one of which he used to keep a choke hold around the neck of a young female slave. An iron chain secured the woman's feet to the wall, and Louis had a tight grip on both her throat and her left arm. Blood poured onto the wooden floor from her left hand. Two of her fingers were missing.

Madame Delphine Lalaurie watched, devoid of any sympathy, as the slave sobbed. Tall, slender, and dressed in fashionable black attire imported from Paris, the attractive Delphine was ten years older than her husband. It pleased her that no hint of gray appeared in the long black hair she kept parted in the middle. It made her look closer to her husband's age, she thought.

Standing between Louis and Delphine was Bruno, their bald, muscular overseer. Bruno played the harmonica with one hand and held the black leather cat-o'-nine-tails in the other.

"I'll be out for a couple of hours, "said Delphine. "I simply must do something with this hair before the party."

Louis frowned. "Can't you stay and give me a hand?"

"I believe you already have hers." Delphine smiled.

Louis's attention returned to his slave. "One more little finger, just one more. Afterward, we'll sew them back on."

Now semiconscious, the slave struggled weakly against Louis's determined grip, but it did her no good. Tears stained her face, and the gag in her mouth muffled her moans.

"Hold still, dammit," Louis ordered.

Delphine walked toward the door. "I wish I could stay and watch, dear. I really do. But I have to do something with this hair."

"I could use some help," pleaded Louis.

"That's an understatement," Delphine said as she fluffed the hair on the back of her head, smiled, and walked out the doorway. Delphine had been thinking about it for weeks. She was going to get some help herself, help to make her own dream come true.

In 1833, the triple spires on Saint Louis Cathedral were still a lower, bell-shaped Spanish colonial style, unlike the tall, pointed French peaks that later generations would come to know. Next to the cathedral stood the great Cabildo, the building where, thirty years earlier, the nation of France transferred the Louisiana Purchase to the United States. Separating the Cabildo from the cathedral was a narrow passage known as l'Alleè des Pirates, Pirates Alley.

Philippe Bertrand, the cathedral's lay sacristan, rented a small, single-story, shotgun-style house in Pirates Alley behind the Cabildo's prison yard. The bright yellow building still belonged to the Cabildo. Until Philippe moved in, it had been used as storage shed. He had heard rumors that Louisiana was planning to sell the land and demolish his humble home to make way for new construction. His brother assured him that, because of the multiple levels of government involved, several years would pass before he could be evicted.

This morning, Philippe had become engrossed in one of his many books, lost track of time, and was now running late. He fumbled with the key while trying to lock the door to his house, then dashed across the alley and used the same key to open the side door to the cathedral. Once inside, he saw that the bishop had already vested for Mass.

Philippe hurried to light two candles on the altar, while noting that the bishop was now tapping his foot, an indication that he was anxious to begin.

Bishop Leo-Raymond de Neckère had just celebrated his thirty-third birthday and appeared both too young and too frail to be leading a diocese the size of New Orleans. The first time he had traveled from his native Belgium to do mission work in America, illness had forced him to return to Europe. It was during his recovery in France that he met Philippe.

As he lit the altar candles, Philippe knew that his tardiness had delayed the beginning of Mass. He knew that the bishop was displeased. Philippe wasn't sure what was causing the bishop to frown this morning, but he assumed it was his own lack of punctuality. He believed the bishop's displeasure was directed at him, and he wished he could escape the present moment.

Philippe could see the expression on the bishop's face. It was more a look of disappointment than anger. A Vincentian rector had displayed the same look when, four years earlier, he suggested that Philippe leave the seminary in France. "You need to decide if you are pursuing a vocation or just trying to escape your pain," the rector had told him.

He had seen the same countenance in his father the day he announced that he was leaving France to sail to America. "You can leave Bordeaux, but the memory will haunt you wherever you go," his father had warned.

As he walked from the altar back to the bishop's side, Philippe thought about the night when, somewhere on the Atlantic Ocean, he got up the courage to ask the man who had only just been appointed bishop of New Orleans if he could be his lay sacristan. He could still see a seasick Neckère puking over the rail of the ship and saying, "That will only feed into your religiosity, but I'm too sick to say no." Three years had passed since that voyage, and now Philippe was standing behind the bishop outside the sacristy door.

Only a handful of parishioners were present for Mass, most of them women wearing the tignon scarves mandated by law for women of color. Among them was Marie Laveau. That the queen of voodoo should attend Mass every morning did not surprise Philippe. Mixing elements of Catholicism with voodoo was common among the free colored men and women who lived in the Tremé district north of the cathedral. Slaves also combined voodoo with Catholic practices, but with far less faith in the words of the priests. Louisiana's Code Noir required slave owners to baptize their slaves Catholics. The slaves, however, often clung to the past, seeking the intercession of various spirits that had been a part of their religions in Africa and the Caribbean. For them, Catholic saints and angels became new manifestations of the ancient loas.

Philippe smiled at Marie Laveau, who was kneeling in her usual place in the front pew. It was common knowledge that the other women of the parish expected to see her there, that they all recognized the familiar single black braid that ran down her neck from beneath her tall red-and-white Madras tignon.

Kneeling near Madame Laveau was Philippe's younger, more muscular brother, Guy. Both the brothers had received the surname Bertrand, their Catholic faith, and their good looks from their father. The similarities stopped there. Philippe always wore white cotton suits—he owned five of them. Guy preferred black vests and American-style work clothes. Philippe was solitary, indeed hermit-like. Guy had used his charm and social skills to build a successful private hook-and-ladder company in a city that still had no municipal fire department. When Philippe spoke English, it was with the thick accent of an immigrant. Constant effort and practice enabled Guy to sound far more like the local French Creole community. "Bonjou," rather than "*bonjour*," and far more often, "good morning."

Philippe was impressed with his brother's determination to learn English. New Orleans now had thirty thousand residents, and the city had been even larger until the recent epidemics. The city was changing, and many of the new arrivals were from places such as Boston and Philadelphia. They didn't speak French and weren't about to learn it.

Another set of "Americans," of course, was the riverboat men, keelboatmen, and the traders from the territories up the Mississippi. They claimed to speak English as well, but as Guy often said, to his ear it might as well have been Zulu or Mandarin. Spanish had once been the language of New Orleans, and French still dominated, but now, in addition to the Americans, Irish laborers, Italian merchants, and even the occasional Slavic sailor were all beginning to speak English.

A cough echoed through the church, bringing Philippe's mind back to the present moment. In the center aisle, a tiny gold reliquary rested on a small wooden table.

Philippe was about to ring the sacristy bell when the bishop grabbed his arm. He could see the bishop glaring at the reliquary.

"I will not celebrate Mass with that sacrilege sitting there," whispered the bishop. "I spoke to the priests about this last night."

Philippe hurried down from the sanctuary to the central aisle, grabbed the little reliquary, and stuffed it in his pocket. He returned to his place by the bishop and rang the bell on the wall to signal the beginning of Mass. The strange little reliquary with its mysterious contents formed a conspicuous lump inside Philippe's suit pocket.

On Royal Street, below the wrought-iron gallery that surrounded the Lalaurie mansion's second floor, four black geldings flicked their tails and bobbed their manes in an effort to shoo away the insects. A glossy black lacquered rockaway carriage waited behind them.

Bastien, Delphine Lalaurie's handsome and trusted coachman, stood by the shiny black carriage wearing a white shirt, crimson vest, and stovepipe hat.

Elise, the petite, eighteen-year-old slave who served as Delphine's personal assistant, was already sitting in the shotgun position of the driver's box.

The Lalaurie mansion's exterior was now pale green and had just two stories, not counting the recessed attic, with its hipped roof and gabled dormers that formed a small third level. Its modest, neoclassical exterior hid a lavish interior and fine imported furnishing. A third-floor addition and countless efforts at remodeling would come in future years, but right now, the mansion was large enough to serve as the setting for some of the most extravagant balls and revelries known to nineteenth-century New Orleans. None of the privileged guests suspected that, in addition to concealing internal opulence, those walls hid a terrible secret.

It was from the depths of that secret that Delphine emerged when the uniformed doorman opened the front door. She approached the carriage and looked at Bastien. "Take me to the cathedral."

Around the corner on Hospital Street, Marthe de Montreuil peeked out the second-story window of the Widow Clay's house.

Old Widow Clay was paying Marthe to be her night nurse, but Marthe spent more time spying on Delphine Lalaurie than attending to her patient. Marthe's husband was Delphine's cousin, and Marthe was obsessed with catching Delphine at something—anything. It was part of a long-standing family feud resulting from an old land dispute.

Taking advantage of old Widow Clay's paranoia and fear of a slave revolt, Marthe had secured a position that would allow her to keep an eye on her rival and report any "suspicious" activity. Her reports sometimes went to the sheriff, but always to the nosy and crotchety old neighborhood gossip, M'sieu Boze.

When Mass had ended, as the parishioners crossed themselves and straggled out of the cathedral one by one, Philippe extinguished the candles on the altar and carried the sacred vessels into the sacristy. The old cathedral's remarkable acoustics carried his voice throughout the church even from inside the that little room.

"Have a nice day, Your Excellency. I will dispose of that item right now."

"Thank you, Philippe. That should never have been displayed without my permission."

"I am sure that whoever the priest was who placed it there thought we had examined it," said Philippe.

Philippe withdrew from the sacristy and was surprised to see Marie and Guy still kneeling in the church. He genuflected and hurried down the aisle, stopping at the small wooden table that sat in the middle of the center aisle. Taking the reliquary from his pocket, he set it on the table and began to open it. A spark struck his hand, causing him to flinch before he removed a small white object from the reliquary.

Philippe took a tiny blue velvet bag from his pocket and placed the object in the bag, then closed the sack by pulling a drawstring. He was careful to keep the bag cupped in his hand once he noticed that Marie was watching him.

"Bonjou, Philippe. What do you have there?" Marie asked as she stood and stepped in front of him.

"*Bonjour*, Marie," said Philippe in a hushed tone. "This? Three ounces of ah… embarrassment. Someone sent it to our bishop, claiming it was a relic of our holy patron, Saint Louis."

Marie looked at the bag in Philippe's hand. "And…?"

"When we examined it, we realized it was a piece of jawbone from a common pig—a…how do you say…a fraud," Philippe replied.

"Playing on the credulity of honest, God-fearing people…"

Philippe smiled. "Says the queen of voodoo."

Philippe and Marie began to walk down the aisle. Marie peeked again at the blue bag in Philippe's hand.

"You know nothing at all about voodoo," she said.

"I know you are the queen," answered Philippe.

"Queen!" she scoffed. "You know I'm a poor old widow who cares for the sick and consoles the condemned, as you yourself should do."

Philippe shook his head. "And you know I'm no minister. I am only here to help the bishop. Old widow! You aren't much older than me."

"You'd be surprised," said Marie.

What surprised Philippe was that Marie was walking to the front door with him. Her habit was to leave Mass by the side door that led to Pirates Alley. She spent her mornings visiting the imprisoned in the yard behind the Cabildo, gathering messages to take to their families, praying with any who were about to be hanged. More often than not, Philippe left by the side door, too. He would try to get into his little house before the prison yard whippings began. If a slave owner had paid to have his slave disciplined, or the court had sentenced some petty thief or prostitute to the lash, he didn't want to see it. He couldn't avoid hearing it. The sounds penetrated his home's bright yellow walls, and he had to read aloud to drown them out. Philippe told himself there was nothing he could do to help those people. He did not want to be anywhere where he might feel the need to protect the helpless.

After all, if I was any good at that, I would still be married.

Guy outpaced Philippe and Marie as he hastened down the aisle. He held up a piece of paper in his hand as he passed his brother.

"Have to file a license next door. See you soon."

Guy's voice shook Philippe out of his moment of self-pity. At least he didn't always have to meet some bureaucratic deadline at the Cabildo. He thought Guy must spend as much time filing paperwork as he did fighting fires.

"What brings you here every morning?" asked Marie.

"I believe in the Resurrection," Philippe replied.

Marie smiled. "But that Resurrection is for those who feed the hungry and clothe the naked. *L'immortalité* of the compassionate. Of course, other resurrections are no great trick. I've performed several of them myself."

Philippe shook his head, dipped his hand in the cherub-shaped holy water font, crossed himself, and opened the door. Marie preceded Philippe out of the cathedral and onto Rue de Chartres.

Once Philippe was on the street, he noticed an impeccably well-dressed woman and her driver standing in front of the church. A light-skinned slave girl was behind them, sitting in a carriage.

"Why the front door today?" Marie asked.

"To get rid of—"

"Marie Laveau," Delphine interrupted, "may I have a word?"

"Madame Lalaurie. May I introduce our good sacristan, M'sieu Bertrand?"

Philippe forced a smile. "Philippe. A pleasure. Very nice to meet you, *madame*." He squeezed the blue velvet bag in his hand. "Now if you'll excuse me."

Delphine reached out, placing her hand on Philippe's shoulder. "M'sieu Bertrand…Philippe…please wait."

Delphine's touch surprised Philippe. He noticed that her attention remained focused on Marie.

"Madame Laveau, I am in need of your services. May I call on you in, say, thirty minutes?"

Marie took a quick look at Delphine's long black hair. "Wanting to look your best for one of your social events? Yes, of course, I will be ready for you."

Delphine's attention returned to Philippe. The expression on her face suggested that she was surprised to find a French-speaking white person in New Orleans she'd never met. "Philippe, my friends have been telling me that the cathedral has a wonderful new sacristan."

"Not so new anymore," Philippe responded. "I've been here for three years now."

"Yes, well, I am so happy that we finally met. Perhaps we can get to know each other better. My husband and I are having a little gathering on Saturday night. Guy Bertrand is your brother, *oui*? I'm sure he will be there."

Philippe supposed that the look on his face betrayed his aversion to social occasions. He knew that the Lalaurie balls were far more than "little gatherings."

"Thank you for the invitation, but I'm not one for social events. I leave that sort of thing to Guy."

Accustomed to getting her way, Delphine was quick to counter Philippe's refusal. "Well then, how about something less formal? Can I persuade you to drop by today for coffee with the doctor and me…say about eleven o'clock?"

Again, Philippe squeezed the little blue bag cupped in his hand and felt a chill come over him. He shivered.

Marie placed her hand on Philippe's shoulder. "Are you all right?"

"I'm fine, just a chill," Philippe said, glancing down at the blue bag in his hand.

"Our house is at 1140 Rue Royale," said Delphine.

Philippe amazed himself when he heard his own voice blurt out, "Ah, *oui*. I will see you at eleven o'clock." Philippe nodded good-bye to the women and walked away.

Marie alone watched as Philippe strode over to a trash bin, discarded the blue velvet bag, and turned into Pirates Alley.

As soon as Bastien assisted Delphine back into her carriage, Marie walked to the trash bin and retrieved the blue velvet bag. She loosened the string and examined the contents.

"Perfect," she said. "From the jaw of a pig." Marie couldn't read books, but she could read people, and she could read the convergence of events as signs from her loas. To Marie, the message was as clear as the written word. She knew what to do.

The walls of Philippe's room were lined floor to ceiling with bookshelves. Two white rosaries sat on a small table next to a copy of M.G. Lewis's *The Monk*. Philippe tossed his skeleton keys on the table next to the book and sat. He stared at the rosaries for a moment, picked them up, and began to slide them back and forth from one hand to the other. The knock on the door startled him, jarring him back from his contemplations. He dropped the rosaries back onto the table, stood, and answered the door. Guy was there, holding two beignets wrapped in paper.

"Good morning," said Guy as he stepped into the room.

"*Bonjour*," Philippe replied as Guy sat at the table. Philippe remained standing.

Guy picked up the copy of *The Monk* that was resting on the table. "This the book you wanted me to read?"

"Scary story," said Philippe.

"Care for a beignet?" asked Guy.

"*Non, merci*. I'm fasting. Just liquids for me today."

Guy looked at the book in his hand. "Oh, one of those days, is it? My brother the monk."

"Monks have to live in community. I prefer my own company."

"I know. The only people you ever talk with are the bishop and our voodoo queen," said Guy as he flipped the pages of the book.

"And you. I talk to you," said Philippe.

Guy helped himself to a beignet.

"You do enjoy Marie's company. Maybe you should marry her," said Guy, now with powdered sugar around his grin. "But, no, that might not be legal."

"Because she's colored?"

"No, because she claims she's dead," laughed Guy.

Philippe smiled. "She does say some odd things at times, but she has a certain *je ne sais quoi*, and she helps a lot of people."

"As we all should do. But that means *being* with people."

"Let's not have this debate again. I admit, attachments aren't always easy." Philippe slid one of the rosaries across the table and put it in his pocket. "You don't remember when Maman died. I do."

"I'm only saying you should get out. You even live next to a dungeon."

"I live thirty paces from the back door of the cathedral. Rather convenient. You live over a…" Philippe paused. He didn't want to argue. "Anyway," he said, "I'm about to leave for a social event right now."

"Really? You're taking my advice?"

"Somehow I was talked into having coffee with Delphine Lalaurie," Philippe explained. "Tried to say no, but something strange came over me."

Guy shook his head. "The Lalauries? Odd. I didn't think they invited anyone unless Delphine was having one of her balls. Brigitte and I only attend those because my company has the fire contract on the place. I should warn you, the doctor is a bit strange."

"I guess I'll see for myself pretty soon," said Philippe.

Delphine Lalaurie weaved her way around the vegetable garden, past the chicken coop and the three-legged dog tied to the pomegranate tree, and up the two wooden steps next to the banana plants. She had been coming to this little cottage on Rue Saint Anne ever since Marie Laveau moved into it nine months ago.

How the voodoo queen had managed to acquire this property was still a matter of much speculation on Sunday afternoons, when folks gathered a block down the street at Congo Square. Some said it was her voodoo; others attributed Marie's good fortune to her prayers in church. Delphine suspected Marie had blackmailed a judge. That's what she would have done.

This modest two-room cottage, with its red tiled roof and single window, was both Marie Laveau's home and beauty parlor for her colored clients…and Delphine Lalaurie.

Upon entering the cottage, the first hint that this was not a typical hair salon was Marie Laveau herself. She carried a large, living, breathing python around her neck. The lit candles on the shelf next to the statues of saints, the dead chicken, and the jars of herbs eclipsed the small collection of the hairbrushes, combs, and scissors.

After a single knock, Delphine poked her head through the door. "Is Zombie in his basket?" she asked.

Marie took the snake off her shoulders and put it in its basket. "All clear now, ma'am," she called out.

Delphine entered the cottage, her eyes fixed on Zombie's basket. "I passed by the French Market to procure some produce. I suppose I'm late," she said, taking a seat in Marie's blue chenille upholstered chair.

Marie waved her hand in dismissal at Delphine's excuse and wrapped a towel around her. As she began brushing Delphine's hair, she spoke her traditional greeting: "Let me work my voodoo on yo' hair."

"Dr. Lalaurie says that voodoo is as ridiculous as the church," Delphine responded.

"Perhaps neither one is ridiculous, ma'am," Marie declared.

Dr. Lalaurie was an atheist. Delphine despised the church but wasn't sure what to believe. If asked, she would reply, "I'm spiritual but not religious." She presumed that some higher power must control things and doubted that anyone could know what it was.

"I don't know, Marie. I don't know what to believe."

"You were going to ask me something last time, but you didn't say what."

Delphine squirmed in the chair. "I needed time."

Marie stopped combing. Delphine wanted to say something. She wanted it more than anything. She had ridden all the way to Marie's cottage to ask for it, but now it felt uncomfortable. Would she sound like a fool? If there was such a thing as sin, looking like a fool must be the most unforgivable sin of all. Still, Marie had opened the door now.

"All right, ah…well…" Delphine hesitated. It was uncharacteristic for Delphine Lalaurie to hesitate about anything. "Dammit, I want to be famous. I want fame."

"I'd say you're already the most prominent and influential lady in N'awlins," said Marie.

"No, Marie," explained Delphine, "I mean the kind of fame that lasts forever. Immortality is more attainable for men, of course, but there have been women with names that live forever…Cleopatra, Joan of Arc."

"Ma'am," said Marie, "as I recall, those two did not come to very pretty ends. Are you sure this is what you want?"

"There must be some, ah…higher powers…that shape our destiny, but can they give me fame?"

Marie walked around the chair and looked Delphine straight in the eye. "If that's really what you want. But fame has a high price, and you must do exactly what I tell you to do."

"I hear you read souls; some say you can even be in two places at once. If following your instructions will make me famous…"

"As you wish," said Marie.

Marie stepped into a back room for a moment and returned holding a blue velvet bag. She handed it to Delphine.

"Take this. Keep it with you at all times, day and night. This is powerful gris-gris, but for it to work, you must come to Maison Blanche on Saint John's Eve."

"By Lake Ponchartrain? At night? No, I don't think—"

"Bring the gris-gris with you."

Delphine was having second thoughts. *A lady of my standing following the instructions of some woman of color? The bayou at night? Perhaps I am a fool.*

"Are you sure your spirits can make me famous?" Delphine asked.

"Ma'am, you deserve it, don't you? I want you to get what you deserve. Something else, you must hide a large bag of gold coins somewhere along the way when you drive out to the bayou."

Delphine scoffed. "So you can steal it? If you want me to give you gold, just say so!"

Marie, accustomed by culture to look downward when addressing white women, lifted her gaze from the floor. It was clear that the voodoo queen was now in control.

"Madame Lalaurie, do not insult me while I am trying to obtain what you desire!" she said with a sudden sternness in her voice. "Like the pirate Lafitte, there'll be a day when you will be glad you hid that gold."

Marie brushed Delphine's hair for another minute before setting down her brush and pulling off the towel.

"There, all finished."

"Already?" asked Delphine. "I do wish you had a mirror."

"Bad luck. You're looking fine," answered Marie.

Delphine stood and handed Marie a coin from her purse. Marie reached into a box by her feet and pulled out a mouse by its tail. She opened the basket and fed the mouse to Zombie.

"I loathe that thing," Delphine said as she walked out the door clutching the blue velvet gris-gris bag in her hand.

Outside Marie's cottage, Bastien was brushing the back end of a horse while Elise sat in the shotgun position in the carriage. Elise was juggling some grapefruit like a circus performer. She had a talent for it. A sudden look of rage traversed Delphine's face when she saw the bright yellow fruit circling in the air. Marie watched from her window.

"Fool girl! Those cost money," yelled Delphine.

Delphine checked to be sure that there were no witnesses along the empty, muddy street before grabbing the horsewhip from the carriage and thrashing Elise across the arm. Three grapefruit fell to the ground, and Bastien dashed over to pick them up. Elise cradled her arm, trying to apologize to Delphine.

Marie's knuckles turned white as she gripped the windowsill. With a groan of disgust, she pushed away from the window, walked over to her chair, and picked up a lock of Delphine's hair from the floor. She stepped over to a lit candle and burned the hair, moving her lips in silence as she recited an incantation.

"Spider!" Marie snarled. May the loas squash you and the darkness devour its own."

Chapter 2

The Lalaurie House

Elise thought the deep lines across Grand-Mère Arnante's withered face made the old woman resemble a roasted pecan. Perspiration stained Arnante's cotton dress and trickled from beneath her white tignon in the furnace-like heat of the Lalaurie kitchen. Arnante had served as Delphine's household cook ever since Delphine's second husband acquired her from the Macarty plantation twenty-three years ago. Had been a time when she picked flowers, when she served dinner to the man who was now president of the United States, but that was long ago. After she tried to run away a few years back, Delphine ordered that Arnante be chained to the kitchen floor. The chain, attached to the shackles on her leg, allowed her to move only about fifteen feet from the oven. She limped a bit now because of an ulcer where the shackles rubbed against her ankle without mercy.

Elise stepped over the chain and around the pile of firewood to hand the grapefruit to Grand-Mère Arnante. Sweat dripped from Dr. Louis Lalaurie's receding hairline as he sat at the table reading the *New Orleans Bee*. Elise wondered why he didn't take the newspaper into the dining room of the main house, where it was at least somewhat cooler.

Arnante cut the grapefruit, placed half in a small bowl, and began to section it with a dull knife, garnishing it with a fresh June strawberry when she was finished.

The door that led to the courtyard swung open, allowing Delphine and a gust of blistering hot air from the patio to enter the kitchen. Delphine tossed her hair. Elise saw that her mistress expected Louis to offer a compliment. It didn't happen. He just cleared his throat and flipped the page of his newspaper.

"Louis," said Delphine, forcing his attention, "the sacristan from the cathedral will be here soon. I invited him for coffee."

"Really?" Louis replied. "I heard he just sits in his room and reads books… never goes out. You haven't started going to church, listening to the shit the priests keep trying to peddle?"

Elise feared that Louis was about to launch into one of his rants about how proud he was to embrace the "enlightened" ideas that had swept across his native France. The word "science" had not come into common usage yet; it was still called "natural philosophy," but Elise and the rest of the household had been told more than once that it would soon replace religion.

"Social contacts," said Delphine, adding, "but some say a little religion might be good for the soul."

Elise had watched Delphine bait Louis many times before. Delphine probably knew her remark would irritate her husband. It did. Louis pounded his fist on the table, and Elise noticed Delphine look away to hide her smile and feign disinterest.

"No such thing as a soul. The secret to life rests in harnessing electricity, not in some priest's incense or some hairdresser's voodoo," roared Louis.

A distant rapping sound emanated from the main house.

"Sounds like Augustine's cane on the front door. Talk to me when you've regained your sense of humor," said Delphine as she stamped out of the kitchen.

Grand-Mère Arnante handed the bowl of sliced grapefruit to Elise, who carried it to the table. Louis pushed it aside.

"Some days she makes me so mad I can't think straight," Louis muttered to himself as he put down the newspaper, stood, and put on a white lab coat that hung neatly folded over the back of his chair. "Elise," he ordered, "come with me."

A look of panic crossed Arnante's face like a cloud speeding across the full moon over the bayou. "Oh no," she whispered.

"Bruno!" Louis hollered.

Bruno materialized in the doorway.

"Tell the pianist to rehearse some Chopin for the ball, and tell him I want to be able to hear it in the attic."

Louis seized Elise by the arm and led her through the door to the main house.

Elise felt dazed and confused as Louis forced her up the staircase. By the time they had reached the landing on the second floor, she considered that the doctor might be planning to rape her. Her mind raced as she struggled to break free. She was tiny, and whatever advantage Louis lacked in muscle, he gained in weight. He covered her mouth with his hand and pulled her up the stairs. At the third-floor landing, he kicked open the laboratory door.

Alarm transformed into pure panic when Elise saw what was inside the attic. She knew she had to escape.

Philippe stepped into the deep-arched white portal that led to the front door of the mansion. The big house wasn't a mansion by French standards, and he suspected Delphine knew that, but in New Orleans, it was large enough to earn that title.

The front door was covered top to bottom with raised carvings of flowers, urns, birds, and the Roman god Phoebus Apollo riding on his chariot. Philippe studied the carvings for a moment before making a fist to knock.

A small green lizard ran up the portal wall to his left. *Anolis carolinensis carolinensis*, Philippe thought. The lizard froze, standing as still as the carvings on the door. Philippe stood frozen, too. The lizard knew by instinct that the shadow of something larger than itself meant it was in danger of being devoured alive. Philippe shared that instinctive feeling as he hesitated at the door. *What made me agree to this? Maybe I should just go home.* The windows at each side of the door revealed somebody moving inside, somebody who had probably seen him by now. Philippe knocked on the door.

Through the glass Philippe saw a uniformed doorman gesturing toward a doorway to his right. The piano music that had been filling the house ceased.

As the entrance door opened, Philippe's downcast eyes gazed at the black-and-white checkered marble flooring of a large foyer.

"Philippe Bertrand," he said, handing his card to the doorman. He was pleased with himself for remembering to bring a calling card. He had not given one out for over a year. "The Lalauries are expecting me," he declared.

To his right and left were open mahogany doors adorned with carvings of flowers and human faces. In front of him was another open door that revealed a long staircase with a mahogany railing. The ornate interior was unlike anything Philippe had seen since he left France. Distinct from most houses on Royal Street, the Lalauries had designed their ground floor for entertaining rather than for storage and shops.

The doorman motioned for him to enter the door on his right. It led to a lavish parlor with Persian carpets, a gilded ceiling, and a fireplace of black marble laced with tones of amber. Fine furniture, imported from France, and large, framed oil paintings on each wall reflected the elegant taste of the woman waiting for him inside. The invitation was for coffee, but she was already sipping a wine that exuded the powerful fragrance of a fine Chianti.

Delphine had that straight, graceful posture of the upper class. She sat across from Augustine Macarty, a distinguished-looking gentleman well into his eighties, who dressed as if it were forty years earlier. His cutaway jacket had gold epaulets gracing its shoulders.

"M'sieu Philippe Bertrand," announced the doorman before returning to the foyer.

"M'sieu Bertrand…Philippe…do come in. Philippe Bertrand, this is my cousin, Augustine de Macarty," said Delphine. "Augustine used to be mayor here in N'awlins."

"We've met," said Augustine, lifting his cane to indicate that he would not be standing.

Philippe shook Augustine's hand and sat.

"Dr. Lalaurie is upstairs," Delphine explained as she pulled a cord to ring for her servant.

"If your husband is seeing a patient…" Philippe began to say.

Augustine chuckled. "Louis doesn't have patients. He claims to be doing research while living well on my cousin's inheritance."

"Now, Augustine," Delphine scolded.

"I also live on an allowance from my family's estate while claiming to help a bishop. I'm sure the doctor's research is a worthy pursuit," said Philippe.

"What's taking that girl?" Delphine grumbled.

In the shadowy attic laboratory, the servants' bell was ringing. Elise fought to get free from Louis, but the doctor had a firm grip on her wrist with one hand and covered her mouth with the other. In one careless moment, he uncovered her mouth to reach for a nearby saw.

"Don't you dare scream!" he ordered.

"No, please!" Elise pleaded.

The bell continued to ring. Louis swiped the saw once across Elise's finger. Blood began to flow from the wound. Elise cried out in pain, pulling and twisting to free herself.

"Madame Lalaurie is calling. I have to go."

Louis lost his grip, and Elise bolted to the door and ran out of the lab and down the stairs, her finger dripping blood along the way.

Louis looked at the splatter of blood on the sleeve of his lab coat. He cursed, pulled off the coat, and tossed it on the floor.

"Where is she?" Delphine complained.

A slave girl came running into the parlor, her finger dripping blood.

"My god, girl," Delphine scolded, "you're bleeding all over my good carpet. What's wrong with you?"

Before the girl could say a word, a man, presumably Delphine's husband, ran into the parlor. He was out of breath. The slave girl trembled as she looked at him.

"I cut myself in the kitchen, ma'am. It ain't nothing," she said.

Philippe stood and bent down to examine the girl's finger. He removed a linen handkerchief from his jacket.

"M'sieu, there are plenty of rags in the trash," Delphine stated. Her voice was cold and dispassionate. "Please do not ruin that lovely linen."

Philippe ignored her. He didn't understand why he had agreed to come here, and now he was feeling something else he couldn't explain. *She's a human being, a real person, and she's hurt.* As he wrapped the girl's finger with his handkerchief, he noticed the welt on her arm.

The young slave's lips moved in silent forming of the words "I don't want to die."

Philippe knitted his brow, not understanding what she said.

"To the kitchen, girl," Delphine's stern voice interjected.

"It's a small cut. You won't die from it. You must be more careful," Philippe said before reminding himself that it was bad form to be addressing someone else's servant.

"Elise!" snapped Delphine.

Philippe looked back at Elise the instant Delphine mentioned her name.

"To the kitchen, now," said Delphine.

"Yes, and bring M'sieur Bertrand a cup of coffee. In fact, coffee for all of us," Louis told her.

Delphine glared at Louis. Philippe's eyes studied Elise as she left the room holding her wrapped finger.

Once Elise was out of the room, Philippe extended his hand to Louis. "Philippe Bertrand, Doctor."

Louis shook his hand as Philippe apologized.

"I forgot that you were a surgeon. I should have let you look at her finger."

Augustine smiled as Philippe and Louis sat. "He's a dental surgeon," said Augustine.

"Now, now, Louis studied in Toulouse. He was a pioneer in France in curing hunchbacks of their deformity," said Delphine.

"Victor Hugo would be delighted," Philippe jested.

"I don't believe I know the man," said Delphine.

Augustine smiled and winked at Philippe.

"The girl's cut appeared to be superficial. I think she will be fine," said Philippe.

"I'm sure it got more attention than it deserved," Louis replied, adding, "They're all so careless."

Augustine lit a Havana cigar. "My cousin was telling me that you might not be coming to the ball on Saturday. You should come. Delphine's parties are the fabric from which legends are woven."

"Yes," added Delphine, "it would mean so much to us if you would grace us with your presence, if only for an hour or so."

Elise returned with a tray holding four French porcelain demitasse cups of coffee and set it before Delphine. She left the room, cradling her bandaged hand. Again, Philippe watched her as she walked away.

"I suppose," Philippe blurted out, "I could stop by for a while, but I can't stay late. Sunday morning Mass, you know."

Philippe couldn't believe it himself. He had just agreed to attend the Lalauries' gala. *Why?* The trail of blood across the carpet answered his question. He realized he had to return to the Lalaurie mansion.

Elise ran to Grand-Mère Arnante in the kitchen, crying now and holding her bandaged finger. Behind the heavy chain that kept Arnante secured to the oven stood Madison, the Lalauries' tall, young footman.

"I seen what they do in the attic," sobbed Elise.

"I don't want to know. I hear the sounds," said Arnante. The old cook had never seen the attic, but she knew she was fixing gruel for somebody up there. She knew Bruno would come into the kitchen sometimes with a shovel, remove her chains, and take her to her quarters. She knew when he brought her back there would be signs of fresh digging in the courtyard outside the kitchen window.

"But, he cut——"

Arnante stopped Elise before she could say another word. "Quiet, girl, or they'll chain you up like me or put you in with the slaves the white folk never see."

Madison unwrapped Elise's finger and exchanged a rag for the linen handkerchief. He began to wash the blood off the handkerchief in a bowl of water.

"But in the attic——" Elise tried to say.

"Whatever you saw, if you want to stay alive, you must never tell a soul. Promise me," Arnante said with a firmness she had never used before with Elise.

Elise kept her head bowed. "Yes, ma'am. I promise."

"Madison, tell this girl," Grand-Mère Arnante said.

Madison looked up from the bowl. "Listen to Grand-Mère. You seal your lips forever, or they'll seal them for you."

Delphine's interest sounded genuine when, after taking another sip of her coffee, she asked, "Tell us, Philippe, how you happened to come to N'awlins?"

"I came with the bishop after he was—what's the word—recovering... recovering in France. He's a frail man; I thought I might be of some help to him. I had recently left the seminary, and my brother and I wanted to see the New World."

"So you never became a priest," Augustine observed.

"No, they told me I was in the seminary for the wrong reasons," said Philippe, unaware that he had pulled a white rosary from his jacket pocket. When he became conscious that he was holding the beads, he worried that Delphine might have seen it. It was, after all, a woman's rosary.

"Do you have any family other than Guy?" Delphine asked.

Philippe looked down, slipped the rosary back in his pocket, and hesitated.

"My father has a vineyard in France," he answered. "My mother died when Guy was born."

"Oh dear," said Delphine, "that must have been most difficult for you. I remember when my first husband died. We were in Cuba."

"I didn't know you were widowed," said Philippe.

"Twice," replied Delphine.

Augustine took another puff off his cigar. "Her last husband was a slave trader, a coffee smuggler, and a pirate. Now she has a surgeon, or researcher of natural philosophy...or whatever."

Delphine gave her cousin a cold stare. Philippe sensed the tension, hurried to finish his coffee, and set down his cup.

"I should be going," he said. "I appreciate your hospitality, and the coffee, but the bishop has benediction this afternoon."

"I should be going, too," said Augustine.

"So soon?" asked Delphine.

Louis stood, and Philippe did the same, assisting Augustine.

"Very kind of you to pay us a visit. I'm glad we met," said Louis as he shook Philippe's hand and walked him toward the door.

"Thank you," said Philippe. "Perhaps Saturday night I can look and see how that poor girl's finger is healing."

"Very good. Until Saturday," said Delphine.

"Madison," Louis called out.

A footman appeared at the door, as if by magic, and escorted Philippe and Augustine out of the parlor. He closed the parlor door behind them and handed Philippe his now damp but clean handkerchief. The handkerchief had been thoroughly wrung out, and that was the exact feeling Philippe had as he stepped back onto Royal Street.

As soon as she saw that the parlor door was closed, Delphine hurled her coffee cup across the room.

"Dammit, Louis," she hissed.

"What?" he asked.

"You fool! He suspects something. After that incident with the stable boy, you promised never to use any slaves who are seen by the community." Delphine wanted to scream at him but wasn't sure Philippe was out of the house yet.

"Yes, he'll expect to see her when he returns. Lapse in judgment. Sorry. I'll find a different subject," Louis said in a meek, submissive tone.

"Well, next time not one of my colored assistants," scowled Delphine. "What's wrong with you? I swear, I am not giving you another picayune for your puddin'-headed research. Do something like that again, and I will divorce you. I will."

Louis opened the door to the library that adjoined the parlor.

"Cleopas," he said to the slave who was dusting the bookshelves, "get a bucket and clean the blood off Madame's carpet."

Philippe and Marie stepped from the cathedral into Pirates Alley after attending benediction. The June sun was baking the sides of the cathedral, but the shade in the alley provided at least some modest shelter from the heat. They walked as far as the lamppost behind the cathedral and stopped.

Marie set down a large, rectangular object wrapped in paper that she had brought to church. Philippe knew it was her picture of John the Baptist, or at least a painting of his head on a silver platter. He knew that Marie would be taking it on its annual pilgrimage to her cabin. He had seen it last year on Saint John's Eve and thought the art was too idealistic, too neat. The artist included just a few drops of blood and gave the Baptist a peaceful-looking face with closed eyes, as if the head were in passive slumber upon the platter.

"You went to the Lalaurie house," said Marie. "I know."

"Yes, but something…" Philippe had a question but was not sure how to ask it. He just said, "Tell me about that girl sitting in the carriage this morning."

"Elise? Fearless. A viper once curled up in her cot on the Macarty plantation when she was nine. Killed it with her bare hands. Why do you ask?"

"Just concerned," said Philippe. "At that house—"

Marie cut him off. "I've never been inside that mausoleum. Other white ladies won't come to the edge of Faubourg Tremé. Wrong neighborhood. They want me to come to their homes, but Delphine always insists on coming to me."

"You suspect something, too, don't you?" asked Philippe.

"What I'm curious about now is why Philippe Bertrand is concerned about another person all of a sudden. Why? Because she's called Elise?"

Philippe's lips and jaw tightened. "Guy must have told you about her. I don't want to talk about that."

Philippe pulled the white rosary from his jacket and began to fondle it.

"He said you'd only been married for a few months and that the men who… did that to her…were never apprehended."

Philippe looked away and began to walk toward his house. He knew that his attempt to learn something about the Lalauries was only going to lead to a discussion about the things he least cared to remember. It was no use. Marie was following behind him.

"You appear to know everything about everybody," he said.

"That's how I became queen," Marie said with a smile, a smile that melted into a look of compassion that Philippe had not seen since he was a child. "Philippe, I understand. First your mother, then your wife. You're afraid to care again."

"It always leads to pain."

"Caring and compassion lead to life, to *l'immortalité*. They are the only path. You may find comfort in the rituals of the church, but religiosity isn't love; it isn't even religion."

"Now I know you've been talking to Guy."

They stopped in front of the little yellow brick shed Philippe called home. He studied the painted bricks, careful not to meet Marie's probing eyes. He knew she was trying to draw him out, to get him to open up to her, but he had closed off that part of his life for too long.

"Did you know that Delphine lost her parents in a slave revolt?" asked Marie. "Since then, people are just objects to her, even more so people who look like me."

Philippe shifted his gaze sharply back to Marie. "And you think I'm like her?" he asked in surprise.

"No, you've both become numb. The difference is that she is hard. Once her daughters left the house, she gave her entire essence to the darkness. You're gentle. You can still care."

Philippe took his skeleton keys out of his pocket and unlocked the door to his house. "I do care," he mumbled.

"Name someone you care about," Marie asked forcefully. "Right now, who?"

"Father Blanc," said Philippe. "He took ill last night. Pray it's not the fever. I have to teach his catechism class until he recovers."

"If you can teach children," said Marie, "think of how many more people you could reach as a priest."

"It's different with children," said Philippe.

"Why?"

"They're young. They stick around, won't all of a sudden disappear."

"Like characters in a book?" Marie's sarcasm did not go unnoticed. "Philippe, I lost eight children to cholera and yellow fever. Love is always a risk, but without love, you cannot have life. You can still give your love to others, but will you?"

With that, Marie waved with a flip of her hand and walked away.

Philippe leaned exhausted against the door, watching Marie's pigtail sway to and fro as she walked down the alley. He felt like he'd had the wind knocked out of him. They'd had conversations like this before, but Marie had never brought up his wife. With a deep breath, he opened the door and stepped back into his solitude. His concern for Elise was proof that his heart wasn't altogether numb. Still, he feared that compassion was something he couldn't embrace, even to save his soul.

Chapter 3

Saint John's Eve

The metronomic beat of Delphine's chair rocking against the hard cypress floor was the only sound in the room. Outside the tall rectangular windows of her second-floor sewing parlor, only the occasional clopping of a horse or mule on Royal Street broke the silence. Most of the wealthier members of the French Creole community had moved to the lake for the summer. Delphine was sitting in the wooden chair caressing the blue velvet gris-gris bag that dangled from her neck. A bullwhip rested on the floor next to her.

The room was hot, and she had asked Madison to open the window. She would be breathing in the night air this evening anyway. It was a risk, she knew, but for fame, it was a risk she would take.

Without warning, Louis stepped out from behind a sliding panel in the wall, startling his wife.

"Damn you, Louis. Use the doors. You frighten me when you come through those panels."

Louis apologized. "I didn't know you were in here. I'm going with Henri to the Saint John's Eve event at the lodge tonight. I was hoping you would change the bandages on Number Five while I was out."

"That's what I bought Bruno for," said Delphine as she stood from her chair and walked toward the door. "I'm going out."

She guessed Louis was too absorbed in his work to ask where she was going. She was right. Now it was time to go. Bastien would be able to find the way. She had allowed Bastien and Bruno to attend Marie's ceremony last year. She knew she could trust them.

Bastien will be with me, and I will take Elise…for propriety's sake. It's not as if I'm going alone.

The road was noisier than Delphine had expected. Frogs croaked, and the loud, annoying buzz of cicadas surrounded them. A full moon was shining through the Spanish moss that hung like an old man's beard from every cypress. The moonlight reflected off the white crushed oyster shells that covered the road up to this point. Delphine and Elise stood by the carriage, looking at a fork in the road. The narrow path to the right, the way they would be taking, was dark and had not been paved with shells.

They found a dry spot along an otherwise swampy roadside. Delphine could see hundreds of footprints in the mud. She realized that had she been here an hour or two earlier, the road would have been filled with men and women headed for Marie Laveau's cabin. Now that the sun had set, the road was empty, and they were alone. Bastien was digging a shallow hole near one of the largest and most conspicuous trees that lined the road. Elise struggled to lift the heavy bag out of the coach.

Bastien helped Elise place the bag in the hole and began filling it with dirt. "Ma'am," he said, "we gonna have to walk the rest. Yo' carriage won't make it down dat path."

Nobody had told Delphine that the road didn't extend as far as Marie Laveau's cabin.

"We will do what we have to do," said Delphine. "But just this once."

Bastien lifted a lantern from the carriage. Delphine knew that she would no longer be in control once they started down that path. Water moccasins and alligators ruled this domain.

The reflection of amber-and-orange flames danced across the water behind Marie Laveau's white painted shack. Built on stilts, the shack rivaled the full moon as it reflected the light from the distant bonfire. An enormous crowd of people, all of them dressed in white, had gathered around the flames. Old rum barrels with animal skins stretched across them now served as conga drums, and the rhythm of drumbeats and jingling of little bells echoed through the swamp. The entire crowd was dancing, spinning in circles. The women waved the hems of their dresses, and the men rocked back and forth in ecstasy, as if they were about to faint.

Marie scaled down the ladder from her little white shack, Zombie, her snake, wrapped around her shoulders. When she stepped off the ladder, she smiled at Elise.

"Come here, girl," Marie said. "You're not afraid of my snake?"

"No, ma'am," answered Elise.

"That's my girl."

Marie waved her arm to beckon the bare-chested young man who served as her assistant at these Saint John's Eve events. He walked over to Marie carrying a vial of liquid and a jar of root powder.

Delphine was nervous and silent, a creature far removed from her familiar habitat.

"Did you bring the gris-gris?" Marie asked.

Delphine remained silent and handed Marie the blue velvet bag. The bare-chested assistant offered the vial of liquid to Marie.

"No," she corrected him, "not the lilac oil, that's for exorcisms. The root powder."

Marie took the bone from the velvet bag and sprinkled some of the root powder on it. She spit on it, put it back in the bag, and returned it to Delphine.

"Now," Marie told her, "if you have done all that I told you, the spirits will grant your wish." She took Zombie from around her neck and lifted him high over her head, crying out, "From this day forward, the name Delphine Lalaurie will live forever!"

"Amen," Delphine mumbled in response.

The flames of the bonfire flared and grew brighter.

Bastien whispered, "Ma'am, you and Elise best come back with me. Y'all not ready fo' the rest of what happens here tonight."

Now almost unconscious, the slave moaned as Louis drilled a hole into his scalp.

Delphine wanted to fan herself, but her hands were full. Louis wiped his brow. The coolness of the morning had passed, and the attic temperatures were climbing like the inside of one of New Orleans's oven vault tombs.

A strange device on the attic's wood-slat floor consisted of a stack of metal plates with a lever attached to them. Wires from this contraption led to a thin metal rod that Delphine was holding while she watched Louis drill into their victim's scalp. The slave moaned in agony.

Delphine focused on the drill. "Sometimes," she said, "when they moan, it's sort of…"

"Stimulating?" Louis asked.

"Well, yes," Delphine purred.

"Hand me that rod," said Louis.

Delphine handed the rod to Louis, who inserted it into the hole he had drilled in the slave's head. Louis pulled the lever on the device. The apparatus emitted a buzzing sound as the man on the table began to convulse and lose consciousness.

"If this works, we'll be famous," Louis said with a smile.

"I want to be famous in my own right," said Delphine, "not because some man stimulated me with his rod."

Louis pulled the lever again, and a buzzing sound preceded a loud zap.

"Damn. I think he's dead."

Fail. Male. In English, they rhyme, don't they? thought Delphine as she stared at the body of the slave strapped to the table.

Louis was frustrated as he pulled the rod from the slave's head and tossed it to the floor. "I suppose I should get dressed for tonight. I wonder if that sacristan fellow will be back," he said.

It was the zenith of elegance in the Crescent City. Hundreds of candles and huge chandeliers lit the ballroom as the violins played. The crowd was in formal dress, some of them dancing, some drinking, and many gathered in little clusters around the edge of the room to chat. Delphine was talking with Guy's wife, Brigitte, who sat on a tiny velvet chair against the wall.

Philippe stood nearby listening to Louis drone on about electricity. He saw Delphine wave to him as she called out, "M'sieu Bertrand, welcome to my world."

"That's what I came to learn about," said Philippe.

Louis stopped his lecture. "Yes, come, let me introduce you to some of our friends," he said. Louis led Philippe over to a bearded young man, probably in his midtwenties. "Philippe Bertrand, this is Delphine's son-in-law, Auguste Delassus."

"My pleasure," Philippe said, noticing that Auguste appeared to be anxious either to get back to his wife or perhaps just to get away from Louis.

"Fine mind for business, that one," said Louis. "Astute, like Delphine."

Louis steered Philippe over to a group of gentlemen who were standing by Delphine and Brigitte. Guy was there, as were Augustine Macarty and two other men.

"Philippe, this is Judge Jean Canonge," said Louis.

Philippe had often seen Judge Canonge heading in and out of the Cabildo, but had never spoken with him. If he had, he might have known that the judge could speak English without any trace of a French accent. He had even mastered the local dialect. Marie Laveau had mentioned that Canonge was smart and had told Philippe that the judge kept a law office on the Cabildo's top floor. According to Marie, he was the most ethical judge in New Orleans, which, considering the tone of her voice when she said it, didn't mean much. Marie said the judge had bad luck at the faro tables around town and had a habit of borrowing money from Delphine Lalaurie to cover his losses. It was a little secret Marie knew about, even if the judge's wife did not.

Canonge lived directly across Royal Street from Delphine, yet supposedly, the man standing next to the judge, attorney Henri Bonnet, always brokered the loans.

"Henri Bonnet, this is Philippe Bertrand, the sacristan at Saint Louis Cathedral, brother to Guy, our fireman," said Louis.

Philippe shook hands with the judge and Henri before Louis added, "Philippe tells me his family are vintners in France."

Henri tapped Guy on the chest. "You never mentioned that."

"I don't think I was ever called to work in the vineyard. That was Philippe's vocation," Guy said with a grin.

"He thinks I should have become a priest, but I'm not good very…ah…very good with people," Philippe explained.

"Nonsense," said Guy. "The bishop asked Philippe to help teach the Bible to a group of children. I'm told he's a great teacher."

"Well," Louis interjected, "let's hope those young ones are bright enough not to accept all that nonsense the Church keep trying to preach. Two of each animal on one boat, talking snakes, parting seas—please."

Guy leaned over to Delphine. "Madame Lalaurie, perhaps before this becomes too heated even for my fire brigade…"

Delphine took her husband's hand and looked around the room. "Darling, look," she said. "M'sieu Higgins is here. We haven't seen him in such a long time."

Delphine led Louis across the ballroom to Higgins. As they reached the southeast corner, Louis exclaimed, "Higgins, how good of you to join us! I didn't realize the circus was in town."

"Delphine! Louis!" Higgins's voiced boomed out with the deep, powerful pitch of one who had been announcing circus acts all his life. "No, the show is down for a week. Hurricane season, wind damage to the tents. So far, it looks as if New Orleans is being spared. Had to bring the equipment here for repairs."

"So sorry to hear," said Delphine.

"Well, that's the circus business," said Higgins. "Always some unexpected expense. Henri told me he was coming here tonight, took the liberty of inviting myself. Hope you don't mind."

"You know you are always welcome here," said Delphine.

Louis was happy to see Higgins. He had been hoping to run into him sometime soon. Last year, he sold Higgins a deformed human skull and dwarf slave. Now, he needed to initiate a more grotesque form of commerce. He'd heard about the tactics Higgins once used to run a Romany circus owner out of Congo Square. He knew Higgins wouldn't ask too many questions.

"I might have a lead on that idea we talked about last year," said Louis. "That should help with some of those expenses."

"You found the half man, half woman? I could make money with an attraction like that."

"Better yet, I may have found"—Louis lowered his voice to a hushed whisper—"a human crab."

"A what?" asked Higgins.

"A human crab," Louis continued. "A girl who walks around face-up on all fours like a crab," Louis exclaimed.

"That's what I need, things people never expected to see," said Higgins. "Where do you find these creatures?"

Louis felt Delphine's nudge and saw her eyes shift toward the man across the room.

"Oh, medical journals," Delphine said. "Yes, medical journals."

Sheriff Eugene Dubois saw Delphine watching him from across the room. He looked away, not wanting to seem too interested. That's when he noticed Philippe.

"Philippe Bertrand. I never expected to see you at one of Delphine's parties."

"Eugene," said Philippe, "I was just getting ready to leave. The Crescent City must be quiet tonight if our esteemed sheriff is here."

"I thought all the rogues and suspicious types were safely locked up in your cathedral," Dubois said with a grin.

"They're always welcome. We let you in every morning, don't we?" Philippe countered.

"*Touché,*" said Dubois. "Oh, I do see a few rogues here: Henri Bonnet—I can't stand lawyers—and that fellow across the room owns a circus. Always a few purses missing when they leave town."

"And the Lalauries?" asked Philippe. "Rogues or good people?"

The sheriff was a better card player than Judge Canonge, and was careful, whenever questioned, not to allow the slightest change of facial expression. His own questions about the Lalauries almost allowed him to indicate something to Philippe, but they were questions based solely on hearsay from Marthe de Montreuil and Jean Boze, the nosy and resentful neighborhood gossips. Nothing had ever turned up to warrant any sort of investigation.

"Well, there are always rumors, perhaps started by those who are jealous of their wealth," said the sheriff.

"Perhaps," said Philippe. "Well, if you'll excuse me, there is someone here I must check on before it gets any later."

Dubois cocked his eyebrow. This was a side of Philippe he hadn't seen before, he thought, as he wondered whom Philippe was in such a hurry to see.

Moments later, Philippe was in the foyer, about to ask the doorman how to get to the kitchen, when, as if by providence, Elise walked by carrying a tray of hors d'oeuvres. Bruno was walking behind her.

"Let's see that finger. It is healing, *oui?*" Philippe asked.

Elise stopped and held out her hand. She glared back toward Bruno and mouthed the words "I ain't afraid."

Satisfied that the cut was healing, Philippe stepped out the door. He was relieved to be back on Royal Street. Bruno looked intimidating, and he was still watching from the doorway. Philippe began to realize that he really cared about Elise, and wondered if he'd see her again.

Chapter 4

Escape

t began as an ordinary summer morning. Delphine sat on a wooden chair in her sewing parlor, looking at the bullwhip that hung from a hook on the wall. Twelve-year-old Leah was standing behind the chair, combing Delphine's hair. Delphine flinched.

"Ouch! Dammit, be careful, girl. You're pulling my hair."

Leah jumped back, and then resumed combing. Delphine flinched again, twisted around, and scowled at Leah. "Dammit, girl, I told you to be careful."

Leah continued to comb Delphine's hair for a minute, but again the comb caught in her hairdo.

"Ow! Leah, I told you to be careful. You pull my hair again, and I will cowhide you like never before. Do you understand me, girl?"

"I's sorry, ma'am," said Leah's soft little voice. Her hands began to tremble, and soon her comb pulled Delphine's hair once again.

Furious, Delphine leaped out of the chair and grabbed the bullwhip from the hook on the wall. She began to chase Leah around the room, whipping her as they ran. Leah screamed, which infuriated Delphine even more. Pitiful pleas for mercy echoed down the halls as Leah dashed through the mansion with Delphine in pursuit.

The sounds of the whip cracking and Leah screaming filled the house. Moments later, the glass of a window on the second floor shattered, and Leah came bursting through the window, onto the wrought-iron gallery. Her dress was shredded and bloody, and her flesh was torn. A flap of skin dangled from her bare shoulder. Delphine continued to chase her, still lashing out with the whip as they ran along the Hospital Street side of the balcony. Leah reached the corner and climbed over the edge of the wrought-iron railing. She teetered on the edge until the whip cracked again across her back. Leah screamed as she plunged from the belvedere into the courtyard below.

"Damn you," said Delphine. "Damn you for going outside."

Delphine saw Marthe de Montreuil staring from across the courtyard. For a moment, but only for a moment, a sense of panic embraced Delphine. She could feel the tension spread across her arms and chest. She realized that her worst enemy had watched the whole scene from Widow Clay's second-floor window. It took Delphine a few seconds before even she could grasp the reality of the grotesque sight in the courtyard below.

Sprawled across a pool of blood, Leah's lifeless, broken body was now silent and still. Marthe disappeared from the window, and in less than a minute, she was out the door and running down the street, probably to summon the sheriff.

Delphine stared back down at the body again, then walked back into the house and checked her hair in the mirror.

Half an hour later, Sheriff Dubois was pounding at the Lalauries' Royal Street entrance. Delphine stood next to the doorman as he opened the door.

"Madame Lalaurie," Dubois began, "Judge Canonge cautioned you twice already. I didn't want to believe it, but now I have no choice."

Marthe arrived at the door. Dubois ignored her. Delphine was actually impressed that the woman could be so bold. The long-standing animosity between the two women was known throughout the Vieux Carré.

"Please do not make this any more difficult for either of us than it has to be," Dubois continued. "This isn't Mississippi. We have the Code Noir. It is illegal to kill a slave here. You'll have to come with me."

Marthe, it seemed, could remain silent no longer. "I heard that one of your servants died," she said, though there had not been enough time for word to get around. "I came to ask if you would like me to take care of the burial arrangements."

"Meddling cow," snarled Delphine. "It's already been seen to. Now go away."

Delphine was telling the truth. The burial had been arranged. Had Marthe remained at Widow Clay's window, she would have been able to see Bruno kicking Leah's tiny body into a pit between the tree and the old well in the courtyard.

The courtroom was dirty and hot. Henri Bonnet sat with Delphine and Louis at one table, Sheriff Dubois and Marthe de Montreuil at another. In the gallery, two of New Orleans's oldest residents, Augustine Macarty and town gossip, Jean Boze, sat separated by an invisible wall of mutual contempt.

Louis complained to Henri, "Government telling a man what he can do with his own property. We need to take this country back, I say. Take it back!"

"Settle down," whispered Henri.

"*Oyez! Oyez! Oyez!*" the bailiff called out. "The Honorable Judge Jean Canonge presiding in the case of Louisiana versus Louis and Delphine Lalaurie. All rise."

Delphine had just made it to her feet when Judge Canonge took his place, rapped his gavel, and said, "Be seated."

Henri knew that Canonge tried to be fair whenever ordinary criminal cases came before his bench. Nothing, however, was ordinary about a case involving Delphine Lalaurie. She was the leading figure in French Creole New Orleans. Considering that, and the other evidence, which included a significant loss at the faro tables and a promissory note handed to Henri on the steps of the Masonic lodge, the judge's decision would be easy.

"Mr. Bonnet," said the judge, "your clients have agreed that they will enter a plea of guilty to the charge of misdemeanor mistreatment of a slave. Is that correct?"

Henri Bonnet stood back up. "That is correct, Your Honor."

"Very good. The plea is accepted. No need for your testimony, Madame de Montreuil," said the judge.

Disappointment gave way to anger on Marthe's face. She stood and stamped out of the court.

"I hereby find y'all guilty as charged. Before I pronounce sentence, I want to tell you something. This offense allows me to impose a substantial monetary fine."

An icy glare told Henri that Delphine didn't like the sound of that.

The judge continued, "However, the Lalauries are upstanding citizens in our fine community, so I am not going to impose the maximum. I am, however, fining y'all three hundred dollars, still no small amount…but certainly far more than that little slave girl was worth to anybody. Dr. Lalaurie, Madame Lalaurie."

Henri stood and gestured to the Lalauries to do the same.

"Thank you, Your Honor," said Henri.

"Unfortunately," said the judge, "given the circumstances, I am also forced to confiscate any and all slaves owned at this time, and order you to surrender them to Sheriff Dubois."

The sheriff stood and walked over to Louis.

"They are to be sold at auction to the highest bidder. To ensure justice, I will conduct the auction myself. Not at a slave market, somewhere quiet. Let's say a weekday at Congo Square. Do you understand?"

Henri and Louis exchanged knowing smiles as Augustine chuckled to himself at the rear of the court.

"My clients understand," said Henri.

"How the hell many slaves are we talking about?" asked Judge Canonge.

"Sixty, Your Honor," said Henri.

"For a household? My god, that's more than some sugar plantations. Very well. Y'all are free to go."

The judge slammed his gavel.

"I don't know why Henri gave them the exact number of slaves," Delphine said to Louis. "Better wash the black ones and feed them."

Even Elise knew that the entire procedure was unconventional. She'd heard that many things Judge Canonge did were unconventional. Delphine said he had once ordered the arrest of the entire Louisiana Supreme Court. The judge lived directly across the street from the Lalauries and was a frequent visitor to the mansion. The Lalauries didn't speak to their slaves very often, except to bark orders at them. Yet, for some reason, Delphine often talked to the kitchen staff about the great Jean Canonge and how fortunate they were to have him as a neighbor. She talked about how he was raised in France, how he prided himself on being able to speak English better than the men in Philadelphia who had taught him to read law. Even Louis talked about how the judge never missed the Saint John's Eve event at the Masonic lodge and claimed he never missed the Christmas midnight Mass at the cathedral.

Today for some reason, the judge had ordered the Lalauries' slaves placed in horse-drawn carts and driven, not to a slave warehouse, but a mere eight blocks directly to the auction. A number of the slaves resisted climbing into the carts at first. Elise understood why. They looked like the dead carts used to pick up the bodies of cholera and yellow fever victims. Maybe they were the dead carts.

Madison helped Grand-Mère Arnante into the cart and climbed in next to Elise. Elise was wearing a blue-and-white gingham dress. She wished it had been a solid color, but at least it was not red.

"They ain't got no dogs," whispered Madison.

"I know," Elise whispered back. "I'm gonna run if I get a chance."

"No, don't run," Madison told her.

"I can't take her whippins no more."

"No," said Madison, "don't *run*. Just stroll away real slow and sit in the brush behind dem trees in the park. They'll be busy looking at me."

"Why?"

"'Cause I'm gonna run. I can outrun dem fat ol' deputies any day...'Sides, so many of us they can't keep track. Sheriff didn't come, two deputies, no chains, no dogs."

Thick bushes and tall live oak trees surrounded the open dirt field at Congo Square. Two deputies in blue uniforms lined the slaves up in rows. Henri moved the darker-skinned slaves to the back rows. They all looked thin and malnourished. Once the slaves were lined up, the deputies just laughed and chatted among themselves, ignoring the slaves.

Judge Canonge stepped onto a soapbox in front of some red, white, and blue bunting that someone had strung between two trees. Above it was a sign that said "Negro Auction."

Augustine looked dapper standing there in his straw hat, tapping his black cane on the hard soil that had been tamped down by thousands of black feet on Sunday afternoons. Like Canonge and Louis, Augustine admired the American experiment in self-governance even if he disparaged the culture, or lack thereof, of the newcomers who called themselves Americans. It was a topic the three men would often be discussing when Elise was called to bring them coffee or, more often, whisky.

Elise was tense now. Her senses became acutely aware of every sight and sound in the park.

"Before we start," she heard the judge announce, "Augustine Macarty wants me to remind y'all that he will be hosting his annual Freedom Celebration on Wednesday, July 4th to celebrate our liberty. Everyone is invited."

Augustine removed his straw hat, leaned on his cane, and bowed to the little group gathered before him.

Elise saw Henri study the rows of slaves. "So many," he remarked.

"Delphine learned from her last husband. Keep a surplus of cotton, sugar, and slaves for when the market is right," Augustine told him.

"Now," Canonge called out, "we'll begin the bidding this afternoon at two hundred dollars."

"For which one of them?" a man in the little crowd asked.

"For the whole lot of them, dammit," snapped the judge.

"Seriously?" asked the man.

It was a ridiculous sum. Beyond ridiculous. It was a downright confession of what was taking place. At a minimum, taking into consideration age and condition, the opening bid for this many slaves should have been closer to fifty-six thousand dollars. One might have thought that every hand would be waving high in the air when Canonge opened the bidding at two hundred dollars. In fact, only one bidder raised his hand until Henri walked over and forced it back down. "You don't want to mess with Delphine Lalaurie," he reminded the would-be bidder.

Madison slipped his hand over his mouth, sliding it back and forth as if rubbing his nose. "I'll distract them," he whispered to Elise. "When they start after me, just walk quiet to dem big trees and sit still."

"I bid two hundred," Augustine called out.

"Two hundred is the bid," said the judge. "Do I hear two fifty?"

The men in the crowd smiled and looked around.

"Two hundred is the bid. Going once, going twice, sold to the Honorable M'sieu Macarty for two hundred dollars."

Right then, Madison bolted away from the other slaves and began to run north. A deputy spotted him and yelled, "One's running away. After him!"

Elise looked around for a moment, nodded, and then began to sneak off to the trees south of her. *I ain't afraid, I ain't afraid,* she repeated to herself, but she was. There could be no turning back now.

A storm was brewing over the Gulf, bringing in dark clouds that helped cool the cathedral even before the sun went down. Philippe stood on a stool dusting off the statue of Saint Patrick at the rear of the church. Alone in the building, he pondered a sermon he had heard Bishop de Neckère once give about Saint Patrick's life as a slave.

The sound of the cathedral door snapped his mind back to the present moment. It surprised him that anyone would be coming to the church at this hour. He was even more surprised when he saw who it was. Elise gasped for breath as she ran up to him.

"You're Madame Lalaurie's servant," Philippe said to her as she collapsed into one of the pews. "What are you doing here?"

"I ran away from the slave auction. Help me, please!"

"You can't do this. I can't do this. You have to go back," Philippe told her.

"Please, m'sieu," Elise pleaded, "Madame Lalaurie's cousin will just return me to that horrible house. You don't know what goes on there. I don't want to die."

"None of us do," said Philippe. "But, I can't..." Elise's words sank in. "Wait, what makes you think you will die?"

"They already killed one girl," Elise said as she regained her breath and stood back up.

"What?" Philippe looked around the cathedral. "We can't talk here. Somebody might see you." He surveyed the cathedral one more time. "Come across the alley with me."

Inside his little house, Philippe pulled up a chair and sat at the table without saying a word. He was as concerned about his own situation as he was about the girl. *What will the bishop say if I am caught with a young female runaway slave in my room?* He stared down at the two white rosaries resting next to a long loaf of bread. *What would my late wife say if I was concerned more for my reputation than a young girl's life?*

Elise probably had not eaten all day. Philippe noticed that the loaf of bread on his table caught her attention as soon as she entered the room. He broke off a piece and handed it to her. A moment later, her interest appeared to shift to the hundreds of books that lined the wall.

"I can't read," said Elise, "but I know about books. I know they got stories and poems and even tell about the past."

"They do have a mystical power," said Philippe.

"Augustine's placée used to read poems to me when I was little," said Elise. "I used to make up new ones in my head and wished I could write them down. You have a lot of books."

"They're how I escape," said Philippe.

"Are they very old?"

"No, but some of the stories in them are," Philippe replied. "That's the magic of books. When a person writes a book, they live on even after they die."

"I wish I could write. Then it would be like you said. I would live even if I die. I want to write even more than to read."

"They sort of go together," Philippe said.

Elise took one of the books off the shelf and pressed it to her heart. Philippe thought she had calmed down enough now to tell him what was going on.

"We can talk about books some other day. The more pressing matter right now is *your* escape. Now, what's all this about killing a girl?"

Elise put the book back on the shelf. "Didn't you hear?" she asked. "They killed Arnante's granddaughter. That's why we were being sold at the dancin' park, but M'sieu Macarty was gonna return us to the Lalauries."

"I suspected something wasn't quite right when you said you cut your hand in the kitchen, but killing a slave is hard to believe."

"Then believe this," said Elise as she twirled around and pulled her dress up to her shoulders. Her back and buttocks were a sea of hideous scars from the whip. Philippe gasped and stared at the scars in shock. Flashes of that terrible night in France mingled in his mind with images of the prison next door.

"I hear corporal punishment being administered every day in the prison yard, but it's done according to code. I haven't seen anything like this since..."

"Since?"

Philippe closed his eyes and gave a slight shudder. "Something that happened in France." His hand shook as he reached out to the rosaries on the table. As soon as he touched one, his eyes opened and his hand steadied. So did his mind. "You're right," he said with resolve. "You have to leave town tonight as soon as it gets dark."

"Where will I go?" asked Elise.

Philippe stood and paced. "I'm not sure...ah...Well, follow the new...how do you say...ah, railroad. No, wait. They will be looking for you. You have to double back toward Congo Square and run to Bayou Saint John. Do you know the bayou?"

"Oui, m'sieu."

"Follow the bayou until you get near Lake Ponchartrain. Madame Laveau has a little white shack out there."

"I know it."

Philippe was surprised that Elise knew about Marie's shack. "Really?" he asked.

"I went there with Madame Lalaurie."

That worried Philippe. "Does she go there often?" he asked.

"Once. She said never again."

"Fine. You can hide there tonight. It is pretty deep in the swamp."

"I ain't afraid," said Elise.

Philippe handed the loaf of bread to Elise, walked to the window, and peeked out. "I'll bring more food in the morning. The sun is starting to set, and it looks like rain. Better get going."

Elise clutched the bread beneath her arm and started for the door.

"Wait," said Philippe, handing her the rosary he was holding. "Take this. It belonged to my wife." He gave Elise a little hug. "Her name was Elise, too," he added.

Chapter 5

Pursuit to Maison Blanche

Augustine and Henri stood with Louis watching Bruno lead the long line of slaves into the Lalaurie courtyard.

"All there but the two who ran away," Augustine said, pointing his cane at the slaves. "Don't forget, you owe me two hundred dollars."

Louis reached into his pocket, searching for cash, but came up empty. "Tomorrow," he said. "I'll talk to Delphine."

"Will you be at the lodge Thursday night?" asked Henri.

"I don't have time for all that occult nonsense," said Louis. "I only go for the social events."

"You sure enjoyed the pig roast in May," Henri remarked.

"More than you know," Louis laughed. "While you were in the chambers doing all that open-grave mumbo jumbo, I took the bone from the pig carcass and sent it to the bishop. Augustine says the damn fool actually kissed it."

"Saw it myself," said Augustine.

"You go to church?" asked Henri.

"Got to protect the public image," said Augustine. "How do you think I kept getting elected?"

Louis and Henri laughed. Augustine's public image was hardly that of a prayerful and virtuous Catholic. The old boy had publicly named his octoroon placée First Lady of the city when he was mayor. The all-male voters, perhaps because of the mayor's zeal to modernize sanitation measures for the city, tolerated Augustine's "left-handed marriage." The voters' wives may not have seen as much humor in his antics.

Once Bruno had all the slaves back inside the courtyard and the snickering about the pig bone and Augustine's supposed piety had died down, Augustine pointed his cane at Louis. "I'll be back for my two hundred dollars in the morning."

Henri helped Augustine into a calèche parked next to the garbage pile outside the carriage gate. Louis saw the rat that was crawling through the rubbish. He hoped his friends didn't notice what it was eating.

Sheriff Dubois paused in front of the parlor window, using it as a mirror to adjust his tie. Madison looked into the window, too. He could see through the parlor to the library where Cleopas, the porter, was handing Louis a drink. Apparently satisfied that his appearance was in order, Dubois led Madison into the mansion's arched portal and knocked on the door. Bruno swung the door open, smirked when he saw Madison in cuffs and chains, and called his master. A moment later, Louis arrived at the door, still holding his glass of whisky.

"I caught this one, and someone reported seeing the female near Bayou Saint John, headed north," Dubois told Louis.

"Bruno, take Madison to his quarters, get the dog and the carriage, and come with us," Louis ordered.

It was a more tolerant reception than Madison had expected, but hearing that Elise had been seen and Louis's order to get the dog terrified him. Delphine seemed to enjoy punishing Elise. If the dog didn't tear that poor girl to pieces, Bruno's whip surely would.

The Spanish moss hanging from the cypress trees blew sidelong with each strong gust of wind, like gray phantoms floating over the swamp. Every few seconds, the clouds blotted out the full moon as they raced across the sky. Lightning flashed in the distance, and the wind wailed as it struck Elise face-on, slowing her pace. She walked along the water's edge, white rosary around her neck, the loaf of bread beneath her arm.

Distant hoofbeats and the barking of the dog alerted her that the time had come. She could no longer avoid the water. She began to run. The barking was getting closer. She tried to pick up her pace, but the mucky bottom of the bayou gripped at her ankles. She struggled to keep her balance but soon tripped and fell. One by one, a group of turtles on a log slid into the water, startled by the splash she made. She stood and began to run again.

Again she tripped, this time falling to her knees. Mud splattered across her dress, but she stood and continued to run.

The sight of the water moccasin skimming across the dark water brought her to a halt. She froze.

Looking back, she could see the carriage carrying Louis, Bruno, and Dubois coming to a stop. The dog strained against its leash. She waded farther into the bayou. The water was getting wider and deeper, and she was already tilting her head back to keep her face above the surface. Something made a loud hissing sound.

The alligator was at least twelve feet long. It slipped all eight hundred pounds of its massive body into the water in total silence. Elise began to cry. The gator swam a few feet from shore before it slipped beneath the surface and vanished.

Elise glanced back toward the shore. The dog's teeth glistened in the flash of the distant lightning. Elise watched as it snarled and barked, jumping and pulling on the leash. When the dog got to the edge of the water, it stopped. Louis, Bruno, and Dubois walked over and stood next to it. Their voices echoed through the swamp.

"That water is only about chest deep on you," Louis told Bruno. "Go get her."

"Master?"

"It's not that deep. Catch her, dammit. Get going!"

Bruno waded into the water and set off toward Elise. She looked back and saw him gaining on her.

The alligator's eyes moved along the surface. Elise took one more step and slipped beneath the surface. She surfaced, spitting and coughing as her arms thrashed about in desperation. Panic and the need for air were enough to cause her to grasp anything she could. A long, dark object moved toward her. She reached out and grabbed it as her loaf of bread drifted away in the current. A moment later, Elise realized that she was hanging on to a floating log.

A flash of lightning revealed that the water was up to Bruno's neck, but he waded in farther. Lighting flashed again, and thunder reverberated throughout the bayou. All at once, the water burst alive with frantic splashing and commotion. Bruno disappeared beneath the surface.

"What was that?" Louis yelled.

"That's now the best-fed gator in Louisiana," said Dubois.

Louis laughed.

"Road ends here," said Dubois. "Want to walk down the trail, see if there's a way across the bayou?"

The doctor's voice sounded distant now. "Not in the dark," Elise heard him say. "The bayou meanders all over back there. Besides, storm's coming. She'll never make it. That water is alive with gators and snakes."

Thunder rolled across the bayou as it began to rain. Despite its grandiose name, Maison Blanche was just a shed. A flash of lightning revealed its presence about eighty feet ahead, nine feet above the ground on stilts. Elise climbed out of the water as the thunder and lightning intensified, and headed for the little white shack. Another flash of lightning showed her that a wooden ladder led to its only opening, a small door with a simple latch and no lock.

She climbed the ladder and slipped inside, leaving the door open. It was too dark to recognize all the items scattered around the tiny room. Voodoo paraphernalia, to be sure, and some candles. Not that she had any way to light a candle, but the first thing she touched felt like a cylinder of tallow. It was too dark to see the mask hanging on the wall until the lightning flashed again. The face was frightening. Some tribal relic from Africa, she assumed. It startled her. Elise grabbed the mask and hurled it out the open door.

She stripped off her wet dress and huddled naked and exhausted in the corner. Her stomach churned, and she wished she had been able to hold on to that loaf of bread. She wondered if Philippe would keep his word, if he would, in fact, be bringing more food in the morning.

The tavern on Rue Saint Philip catered to a more refined clientele than most such establishments in the Vieux Carré. The owner had overcome the prejudice against Italians by serving only the highest quality food and beverages. He served from the bottle, not from a barrel. In the daytime, you could even get coffee and home-baked biscotti. "My mother's recipe from Italy," the bartender would always say. The Creole gentlemen who frequented the place were more accustomed to drinking bourbon or sipping the green fairy than to ordering coffee and biscotti.

Tonight, the place was empty except for the bartender, who was wiping the bar. It didn't need wiping, but he needed something to do to stay awake. His half-closed eyes opened to the sight of lightning flashing as the door sprang open. He caught a glimpse of the hard, steady rain blowing sideways down the street before the door slammed shut again and Philippe ran past him.

"Well, look who the devil dragged in," he said. "I don't think your brother—"

"Some other time," Philippe mumbled as he pulled a set of keys from his pocket and dashed up the stairs at the rear of the bar.

The bartender was surprised to see Philippe, especially at this hour. He knew the sacristan didn't like to come to St. Philip Street, knew that the fire hall reminded Philippe of his wife's murder. The young bride had gone alone to see an exotic animal, something called a giraffe, that was traveling on royal exhibit across France. She never returned home. Local farmhands found her slashed and mutilated body in a ditch and followed two sets of bloody footprints until they disappeared into a vineyard. The tale of her grisly death was well known to the patrons of this saloon, but it was never discussed around either of the Bertrand brothers.

Philippe's wet suit coat dripped on the floor, leaving a puddle at his feet as he stood in the dark parlor above the bar.

"Guy? Brigitte?" he called out.

Brigitte sounded more curious than alarmed when she responded from the next room. "Philippe?"

"Where's Guy?" asked Philippe.

Brigitte stepped into the parlor wrapped in a blanket. She lit a candle as Philippe put his skeleton keys back into his pocket.

"Across the street," said Brigitte.

The building across the street bore a sign that read "Fleur de Lis Hook-and-Ladder Co."

"Guy went over there about an hour ago," she said. "Lightning struck a house on Rue Bourbon, but I think the rain probably did more than Guy's fire brigade to put out the fire. I heard the equipment returning to the fire hall a little while ago."

Philippe refused to set foot inside the fire hall. Its wide arched carriage entrance and the building's faded mustard color both reminded him of the mortuary in Bordeaux, the mortuary where Guy and his father had pleaded with him not to view his wife's body.

Guy insisted that the fire hall looked nothing like that building in Bordeaux, but they looked the same to Philippe.

"I'll signal him," said Brigitte.

Brigitte opened and closed the curtains twice, then took Philippe's wet coat and wrapped a blanket around him.

"So what got you out of your tomb…and at this hour?" she asked.

"You need to get better locks. The keys we use at the church open half the doors in this city."

"They say locks are for honest people," said Brigitte. "Most of the neighborhood doors will open with one of three common keys."

Philippe pulled the white linen handkerchief from his pocket and sneezed.

"If this rain doesn't give you pneumonia, the night air will give you the fever," warned Brigitte, shaking her head. "Now, what's this all about?"

"I need your help," said Philippe.

The apartment door swung open, and Guy rushed into the parlor, asking his wife what was wrong before even noticing that Philippe was standing there.

Philippe looked at his brother and took a deep breath. "I'm about to harbor a runaway slave, Delphine Lalaurie's servant girl. She's been abused, subjected to horrible beatings."

Philippe and Brigitte stood speechless for a moment before sinking into the chairs at their table. "Did you tell the sheriff about the abuse?" asked Guy, with a look that suggested he was still trying to comprehend what his brother had said.

"How can I do that without betraying the girl?" asked Philippe. "He'd arrest her."

Brigitte's face pleaded in silence for Philippe to abandon his plan. "Harboring a runaway. Do you understand what that means? The risk?"

Philippe was silent. He gazed at the floor. Guy took Brigitte's hand.

"You need to be careful before you accuse the Lalauries of anything," Brigitte said. "Delphine has money and power. She's related to half the Creole community. She'll crush you if she feels threatened."

"Brigitte is right," said Guy, who must have known that a confrontation with Delphine would spell an end to his business, as well.

"I think something worse than beatings is happening in that house. I just don't know what it is. Elise said she cut herself in the kitchen, but I know I heard her running down the stairs."

"Her name is Elise?" asked Guy.

"Oh, my," sighed Brigitte.

Guy squeezed Brigitte's hand as Philippe had often seen him do before when coming to a decision. "Well, we'll need some sort of evidence before you can go to Dubois."

The slave on the laboratory's cypress-beam floor had his feet chained to the wall and a tourniquet wrapped around his right arm, which was amputated at the elbow. Lightning flashed through the attic shutters as Louis stooped down to connect the wires. Delphine's shadow flickered across the floor with each burst of lightning through the window.

"Maybe I don't have the right amount of current," said Louis.

"I don't understand any of it," Delphine replied.

"It's called Galvanism," said Louis.

"Calvinism? You're an atheist."

The lightning flashed again.

"Galvanism!"

"Calvin or Galvin, what's dead is dead. After that, the only immortality is fame," Delphine declared.

Louis attached an electrode to the wire. He touched the electrode to the severed arm on the floor and threw a switch. The arm twitched for a moment.

"In France, Dr. Lefebre and I made a severed limb move, but I am on the verge of bringing one back to life," Louis declared.

"Dr. Lefebre, Dr. Lefebre. Honestly!" Delphine scoffed.

"Delphine, think of what this will mean to the troops on the battlefield. We will be famous," Louis replied.

"I believe I…I…will be famous," said Delphine as she touched the blue velvet bag that hung around her neck. "That I believe. What I do not believe is that you can attach that arm. It already stinks."

Louis examined the slave. "Gangrene has set in," he said as he wiped his brow and unbuttoned the top button of his shirt. "That was fast. I'll have to cut it again."

The slave began to moan and shake his head in protest.

"I hoped that by removing his limbs and reattaching them backwards I could produce that crab boy I promised Higgins," said Louis.

"You fool!" Delphine cried. "You told Higgins it was a crab *girl*. No point in trying to save this one. How long does it take to die from gangrene, anyway?"

"Not sure," said Louis.

"Well, let's find out. At least you'll learn something."

Philippe and Brigitte were wedged in next to Guy as their buggy carried them over the bleached shells that covered the bayou road.

The sky was clear now, but travel was slow. The previous night's storm had left patches of mud that clung to the wheels of the buggy. Philippe sensed that the road itself was trying to keep them from reaching their destination. The horse was straining to pull the buggy out of yet another mud patch when they spotted Marie, riding on a mule. Philippe called out to her, and Marie's mule came to a stop.

"I am praying to find somebody I sent to your shack last night," Philippe said when they caught up with Marie, "and we need your help."

"I'll always work my voodoo for anyone who is desperate," said Marie with a bewitching smile.

"Marie, this is serious," said Philippe. "We have to trust you."

"That buggy ain't gonna make it all the way to my place," Marie replied. "My mule can get down the path, but y'all will need to walk some."

When they arrived at Marie's shack, Guy tied the mule to a tree, and Philippe handed a large bag he had been carrying to Marie.

"Food and dry clothes," he said. "I got them from the Ursuline Sisters this morning."

Marie picked up the mask from the wet ground below the shack and climbed up the ladder. Philippe could hear Elise moving about in the shack above him. No doubt, the whinnying bray of the mule and the sound of voices had awakened her. Marie remained on the ladder and poked her face through the doorway.

"It's all right, girl. It's Madame Laveau. You're safe," Marie assured her as she placed the bag and the mask inside. "Come down when you're ready."

As she stepped off the ladder, Marie motioned to the others to follow her. She walked to the water's edge and stopped by a small wooden pirogue that rested in the Louisiana muck.

"Y'all picked a good place to send her," said Marie. "Nobody ever comes this far into the swamp."

"What about the voodoo?" Philippe asked.

"Once a year, on Saint John's Eve, in order to be by the water. Even on those occasions, nobody dares to look inside my cabin," said Marie. "I'd like to have ceremonies here more often someday, but for now, I figure once a year is all the authorities will tolerate."

Philippe nodded in agreement.

"Fearless, isn't she?" said Marie as Elise climbed down from the shack.

"And *trés* intelligent," said Philippe. "She wants to learn to read and write."

Even Marie could not read or write. She always signed her name with an *X*, three *X*s, in fact, always pronouncing "Marie...Laveau...Paris" as she made the marks.

"I can't stay out here with her," said Marie. "She'll be alone most of the time."

Elise, now wearing a simple yellow dress that Philippe had brought, joined the group. "I ain't afraid of bein' alone," she said.

"That's my girl," said Marie. "All right. No flames at night, but there's a sack of lemongrass under the shack. Sprinkle some on the embers if the mosquitoes get too bad. We can bring food to you. There's already plenty of crawfish out here."

"And I'll come to teach you to read," said Brigitte.

"Y'all can go to prison for teaching me to read," said Elise.

"Or just for hiding you here," Marie said. "Come now, I need to move this boat up under the shack."

As Philippe and Guy took hold of the pirogue and began pulling it toward the house, a large crab crawled out from underneath. Marie picked it up.

"Dinner!" she said, carrying the crab over to an upright log and picking up a mallet.

Panic filled the dark, watery eyes of the slave girl chained to the table. A muzzle muffled her desperate pleas. Louis stood over her holding a mallet. One of her arms dangled off the table, broken at a peculiar angle. Delphine stood next to the table, holding her other arm. A rectangular block of wood rested at Delphine's feet.

Louis raised the mallet in the air and slammed it downward with all his strength.

"What are we doing?" Delphine asked.

"Making a crab girl," said Louis.

Delphine picked up the block of wood from the floor and placed it behind the girl's knees. Louis could not help noticing that Delphine looked aroused as the mallet came smashing down once more. The girl lost consciousness when it broke her knees with a sickening cracking sound.

"Let's eat," said Louis. "Afterward, all I have to do is reset those limbs facing the opposite direction. In a few months, I will have taught her how to walk on them."

"That's not exactly reanimation," Delphine declared.

L'immortalité

"This voltaic cell is too weak, and copper and zinc sulfate are expensive. I need to sell her to Higgins."

The girl on the table regained consciousness and moaned.

"But she's bound to tell Higgins what happened," warned Delphine.

"Not after I cut out her tongue," Louis replied.

The slave girl fainted.

It was past midnight. Philippe studied the stable's wooden wall as best he could in the dark. He searched for a weak spot in the timbers that might permit entry, but there didn't appear to be any. The stable that stretched from Widow Clay's house to the Lalaurie mansion wall was solid, well built. He moved to the carriage gate to his right. It stood as an extension of the fortification that formed the Hospital Street side of the mansion. Philippe hoped that the gate would not make too much noise if he could get it open. He need not have worried about that. The gate was locked.

The sudden growling and barking of a dog inside the courtyard caused Philippe to back away from the gate. The muscles in his arms grew tense. Not only was the Lalauries' dog sounding an alarm, Philippe knew it could be released through that gate at any moment. *This was a foolish idea.*

Philippe crouched down next to a pile of garbage and cringed when he saw a rat crawl past his hand. The balcony overhead prevented him from seeing clearly, but through the cracks it appeared as if candlelight were now glowing from a second-floor window. He crept on his knees past two arched windows beneath the gallery, stopping when he heard the sound of footsteps. *Whoever you are, please don't turn the corner.*

Looking up, he discovered that he was kneeling beneath a poster affixed to the side of the mansion.

TEN-DOLLAR REWARD

RUNAWAY, the Negress ELISE, aged about 18 years. Speaks French and English. The above reward will be paid to whoever will lodge her in jail, and give information thereof at the office of
Sheriff Eugene Dubois.
Captains of vessels and all other persons are cautioned against harboring or employing said Negress, as the law will be rigorously enforced against all so offending.
July 5, D. Lalaurie

Dubois rounded the corner from Rue Royale. "Philippe Bertrand. What the hell are you doing?"

"I've got a stone in my boot, just trying to remove it," said Philippe as he looked up at the sheriff.

"Balderdash. I don't know why you are sneaking around here, but you'd better be careful. Lalaurie loves all things military and has an impressive collection of guns."

Philippe got to his feet.

"A lot of folks are leaving town because of the fever," the sheriff continued, "but the Lalauries are sticking around, so don't come back."

"Sheriff," Philippe began to explain, "I think they're doing something illegal."

"Like what?" asked Dubois.

"That's what I was trying to find out. Something worse than beating the slaves."

"Yes," said Dubois, "they killed one. That's already a matter of court record. Nothing more you or I can do about it. Do you have any new evidence, witnesses?"

"None to speak of."

"Then drop it. You're startin' to sound like Old Man Boze. The case is closed. Now, go home where you belong and leave the police work to me."

Perhaps he is right, thought Philippe. *Perhaps all I can do now is care for Elise.*

"Besides," said Dubois, "you shouldn't be breathing the night air at this time of year. It carries the pestilence. There have already been quite a few deaths in Faubourg Marigny, and it hits immigrants like you the hardest."

Chapter 6

September Death

The next eight weeks were hell. Philippe made at least twenty trips out to the bayou, but only during the day. Most of his time, however, he spent caring for one sick priest after another. The fearsome epidemic that covered the faces of its victims with an eerie orange mask had descended over the rectory like a holocaust sent by Satan himself. It hit the recent European immigrants hardest. The Americans also lost hundreds. The French Creoles and the colored men and women, both freemen and slaves, experienced fewer deaths. Among the African blacks, most deaths were infants and toddlers.

On the fourth day of September, the disease unraveled the one knot that had been holding Philippe's life together. That morning, the scourge of yellow fever spit in the face of all of Philippe's prayers and carried the immortal soul of Bishop de Neckère into eternity. De Neckère's hours of agony and delirium were over. The person who had brought Philippe to this sweatbox they called the Crescent City, the only reason Philippe could give for being here, was gone. A quiet moan, a tiny bit of coal-black vomit, a final opening of the eyes, and he was gone.

Once everyone had taken their turn shuffling past the catafalque, once everyone but Philippe and Marie had left the church, tears streamed down Philippe's face. He couldn't bring himself to leave the coffin. He stood there in silence with Marie at his side. After a few minutes, he made the sign of the cross. Marie adjusted the blue scarf that graced her neck, the one she wore for funerals, before taking out a white handkerchief and following Philippe down the aisle toward the cathedral door.

"He was a good man," Marie whispered. "I saw him visiting the fever victims before he caught it himself."

Philippe was silent. He wished now that he had gone with the bishop to comfort some of those victims.

"I've lost count," said Marie. "How many priests has it claimed this year?"

"Five," said Philippe.

"Terrible, though not as bad as the cholera last year."

Marie was right. The cholera epidemic of 1832 had killed six thousand people, one-sixth of the city, in only three weeks. Cholera, unlike yellow fever, did not spare the darker-skinned population. It was very much an equal-opportunity killer.

The cholera plague was gone, but this year another disease had come to take its place, carried, they said, by the night air. Whatever the cause, it had just claimed the life of Philippe's bishop.

"I'll see you this afternoon at the cemetery," Marie said once they had stepped out of the cathedral.

"No," said Philippe, "he's being buried here in the cathedral."

Bishop de Neckère would be the first bishop laid to rest in Saint Louis Cathedral.

"Meet me in the cemetery at four," Marie repeated.

The firmness of Marie's command caught Philippe off guard. It was as if she knew this was her time to act, to draw him out of his solitude and into life. He didn't know how to respond.

Marie's tone softened as her hand met his shoulder. "There are lots of others to console. The only reason you've had for being here is back in that coffin. Time for you to embrace the living, if life is what you truly want."

The cemetery chapel could hold no more. The bodies now lined the cemetery wall, forming a levee built of decaying flesh wrapped in maggot-infested cloth.

Father Antoine Blanc read prayers and sprinkled holy water over each of them. A dense cloud of flies buzzed around the stack of white-swathed bodies while twisting trails of ants moved in to feast.

Most of the bodies were unattended, but pockets of mourners wept over some. Marie made her way from family to family, praying with them and extending what small comfort she could offer. Philippe watched for a while before following her lead.

Marie kept the white handkerchief she held at her side. Philippe used his to cover his nose and mouth in a futile attempt to block the stench. Father Blanc did the same.

Marie pulled a small vial from her pocket and poured a few drops of something onto Philippe's handkerchief, then did the same for the priest.

"Yes, that helps," said Philippe.

"Jasmine," observed Father Blanc. "Now my handkerchief will smell like a Canal Street prostitute." With a sly smile at Philippe, he anticipated the how-would-*you*-know question. "The confessional screen only prevents me from seeing the penitents, not from smelling them."

"Does this fever epidemic frighten you?" Philippe asked Marie.

"No," she said, "because if I die, I will rise again."

"That's true," said Philippe as he swatted a mosquito. "We will all rise again on the last day."

"I don't plan to wait that long," said Marie.

She led Philippe farther back into the cemetery, stopping in front of a Greek-styled tomb that bore a plaque engraved with the number 347. She leaned against the tomb.

"Yes," said Marie, "someday Baron Death will put my bones in one of these tombs." She paused to take a stone from her pocket and used it to scratch an *X* on the tomb. "But if they open it a few days later, I won't be there. I'm destined to return."

"Ridiculous," said Philippe. "As what? A zombie?"

"Not in the sense that you mean," Marie replied. "Anyway, you wouldn't know a zombie if you saw one."

Marie knocked on the tomb three times. Philippe thought he heard her whisper, "Father, Son, and Holy Spirit."

"Come with me," she said as she made her way past whitewashed sepulchers and graying statues that were as silent as the bones beneath them.

Philippe and Marie walked down Rue Conti side by side. The familiar odor of sun-drenched horse piss on the street now replaced the stench of the cemetery. A horse-drawn dead cart filled with more shrouded bodies passed them on its way to the burial ground.

"I respect your sincerity," said Philippe, still thinking about what Marie had said a moment ago, "but Saint Paul wrote, 'It is given to man to die but once, and after that the judgment.'"

"What about Lazarus?" asked Marie. "Did he die just once?"

"Well no, but..."

"A few who failed to do enough good in life come back to atone," said Marie. "I was sentenced to be my own bokor."

"I don't know what that means," said Philippe, "but the only zombie I believe in is that snake of yours. That is his name, isn't it?"

They stopped for a moment, standing by a poster pasted to the side of a building.

Coming Soon
Higgins Circus
See the Amazing Crab Girl

"Zombies!" Philippe scoffed. "So you will be a rotting corpse that walks around all stiff legged and thirsting for blood?" He adopted a distant stare, tilted his head, and took a few mocking steps with his arms out straight.

"That's for children's campfire stories. You're acting silly, and you have it all wrong."

"Then what are you saying?"

"I'm like a stick tossed into the Mississippi, sentenced to wash up on the riverbank many times before I go out to sea," Marie said in a sad, serious voice.

"Reincarnation?" asked Philippe.

"No, not coming back in a new body. We only get one. To live forever would be hell, to live in eternity, heaven. There's a difference."

"You puzzle me," said Philippe. "Sometimes I think you understand the scriptures better than anyone in our parish, and other times I don't think you understand them at all."

"I was about to say the same thing to you…until you met Elise."

Philippe's thoughts reverted to Elise. "One of these days I have to ask her—"

"No!" Marie said with a sudden firmness in her voice. "She's buried the stench of those memories. Don't make her dig them up again."

Sheriff Dubois left the Cabildo and was stepping into Pirates Alley when Philippe came out of the cathedral. Dubois caught up with the sacristan and extended his hand.

"Sad business about the bishop," said Dubois. "I know you were close, just wanted to express my condolences."

"Thank you," said Philippe. "I wish you had been as concerned when that little girl died at the Lalauries'. Twelve years old, and they walked away with a slap on the wrist."

"Philippe, I did my job as best I could. Blame that attorney Henri for how things turned out."

"Sheriff, the Lalauries—"

Dubois held his hand up. "I've heard all the rumors. He beats her; she beats a daughter, smuggled black ivory from Africa and Dominique. I need proof, not feelings, not rumors. Without proof—"

"And if, someday, I bring you proof?" asked Philippe.

"I'll act. She doesn't hold my mortgage. But I've warned you before; don't try to become an amateur detective. You belong in the seminary, not the police force."

"This has nothing to do with the priesthood," Philippe sighed. "How can you tell me to enter the seminary but ignore my gut feelings about the Lalauries?"

"Philippe," Dubois said as he pointed a finger in Philippe's face, "understand me when I say the Lalaurie case is over, done. Horrible whippings happen on the sugar plantations all the time, law or no law. Let it be."

Marie said the same thing. But can I?

Louis knew that the Louisiana heat consumed a body in less than a year inside the oven vault tombs of Saint Louis Cemetery. *They wouldn't last much longer up here*, he thought as he bent down to open the shutters in the attic. His shirt was stained from sweat. *I probably smell like a tomb.*

Delphine fanned herself, bent down, and closed the shutters that Louis had just opened.

"How many times have I told you to keep the shutters closed?" she snapped.

"It gets like an oven up here," Louis said in his own defense. "Will this heat never end?"

"The heat and the pestilence are both bad this year," she admitted. "Let's go to Mandeville till it cools off. We haven't been all summer."

Louis twisted some wires together. He was the one who had insisted on staying in town this summer, a departure from their normal habit of heading to the lake no later than mid-June. He thought he was about to make a breakthrough. He had hoped that by now he would be writing to Dr. Lefebre to announce the successful reanimation of dead tissue. Instead, nothing was working. The wires he had just connected came apart in his hands. He tossed them against the wall.

"We may as well go," he said. "This isn't working."

Delphine snapped her fan shut and smiled. Louis took off his blood-spattered lab coat and tossed it on a table caked with congealing body fluids and covered with flies.

It was the humidity that finally forced Philippe to remove his suit coat. He noticed that the heat had done nothing to reduce the number of people who showed up at Congo Square this Sunday afternoon. It only served to increase sales for the woman who peddled lemonade to the spectators. Like many others, she sold things here on Sundays in hope of saving enough money to buy her freedom one day.

The crowd included a few white visitors from other states. More than their accents, it was the astonished looks on their faces that revealed them as visitors. They were surprised that this Sunday gathering of slaves was, for the most part, unsupervised. In fact, they were amazed that the city permitted such a gathering at all, not to mention playing African music. Such things were unheard of in the neighboring Protestant states and territories. Like burying blacks and whites in the same cemetery, it was all unique to New Orleans.

Local French Creole men came for the titillation of watching the calinda and other dances that they considered too exotic for their wives to see. The sheriff came to satisfy those who feared these weekly gatherings could breed revolt. No small number of immigrants and free people of color came to meet with the woman who was dancing in the middle of the square, the one with the snake wrapped around her shoulders.

Just as the Champagne balls at the Lalaurie mansion served to enhance the power and influence of Delphine Lalaurie, the dancing at Congo Square enhanced the power and influence of Marie Laveau. Philippe knew that here she was indeed the queen. He remembered that once a year, on the last day of October, Marie left an offering of corn in the square for the spirits of the Houma Indians who had once used this ground to trade their goods. It was her way of thanking them for their blessing. It was their spiritual intercession, she said, that had changed this plot of land from a whites-only circus venue to a place her people could enjoy, a place where she could dance.

This afternoon, Marie swayed with a slow, deliberate, motion. Her feet never moved, while her body appeared to float beneath her thin white dress.

When the beat of the drums and ringing of bells and tambourines stopped for a while, Marie walked over to a woman selling pralines who was keeping an eye on both of Marie's baskets.

Philippe recognized the praline vendor as a prominent voodooienne who sold herbs and potions from a small house on Saint Peter, just off Rue Royale. Her skin was so light she could pass, and that might have helped her get the house on Saint Peter. She could sell her own potions from that house, but here at Congo Square, she worked for Marie.

She slid Marie's baskets over to the voodoo queen, who placed Zombie in one basket and began to remove various colored gris-gris bags from the other.

Philippe watched as a heavyset man approached Marie.

"Madame Laveau," the man pleaded, "I need your help."

Marie cupped the man's hands in her own. "It's about your wife, isn't it?" she asked.

"Why, yes. Yes, it is," said the man, who now appeared to be convinced that everything he had heard about the voodoo queen must be true.

"I'm afraid your suspicions are correct. She is being unfaithful. It's that Spanish cobbler who lives down the street."

"I'll kill him!" the man shouted before noticing Sheriff Dubois was standing less than thirty meters from him.

"No," Marie advised in a calming tone. "Take no revenge. Instead, I want you to do this…" She whispered something in the man's ear.

He blushed and grinned. "Oh, Madame Laveau!"

"Of course, it works better if you place this under your mattress," said Marie as she held out a red gris-gris bag. "Powerful gris-gris," she said, "and *hard* to come by."

The man handed Marie five silver dollars, took the little red bag, and walked away smiling.

Philippe walked over to Marie wagging his finger at her. "Is that your voodoo?" he asked. "Just a cheap Gypsy trick I used to see in France."

"M'sieu Bertrand!" said Marie with sudden indignation.

"I'm sure a hairdresser hears more confessions than the priests at the cathedral. Plus, half these slaves tell you whatever they overhear in their masters' homes. Nothing supernatural about that."

"The power of the spirits is very real," insisted Marie. "Perhaps I help them along, but it's real."

Philippe knew that voodoo was an ancient religion, sacred to those from the islands and from Africa who practiced it. He also knew that Marie was beginning to modify the cult by introducing new elements, such as veneration of the Virgin Mary. What bothered him was her use of a network of spies to convince others that she had supernatural powers.

"Do you claim you are contacting some loa?" asked Philippe.

"Does it matter if a person prays to Saint Patrick as patron of the enslaved or kneels before the same statue and calls him by another name?"

"Is that what you do?" asked Philippe.

"No, I believe that only a priest reaches to the Good Maker, but the loas hear every invocation. Dr. Lalaurie doesn't believe it, but even the rituals at his lodge are heard by certain spirits and can affect the things around us."

Marie had made an interesting comparison, Philippe observed. Like the deists who dominated the Masonic organizations in New Orleans, the practitioners of voodoo did not believe that the Creator paid attention to human affairs. It was the reason why voodoo sought only the help of lesser spirits. A lifelong Catholic, Marie allowed that the Creator did listen to the petitions of a priest during the Mass.

"God hears all our prayers, not just the priests'," said Philippe.

"Well, someone heard one of yours. The Lalauries left yesterday for Mandeville," said Marie. "If you still want to get into that house…"

According to Marie, Bastien kept most of the slaves locked in their quarters above the kitchen whenever the Lalauries left town. Madame Laveau's spy network was quite reliable. They said that Bastien, knowing that he had secured the servants, had grown careless about locking the carriage gate at night.

Philippe was pleased when he found the report to be true, and the gate unlocked. He opened it enough to slip into the courtyard, crept past the bougainvillea that climbed the pillars of the stable to his left, walked between a tall tree and an abandoned well, and stepped up to the brick-paved terrace outside the kitchen. It didn't surprise him that one of his keys opened the old lock on the kitchen door. He remembered Brigitte's words. "Most of the neighborhood doors will open with one of three common keys."

Inside the dark kitchen, the only light came from the embers burning in the oven. It provided just enough illumination to keep him from tripping over the fifteen-foot chain that stretched across the floor from the oven to the woodpile.

Philippe picked up a candle from the table and lit it by blowing on the embers in the oven.

Beeswax, like we have for the altar.

Philippe made his way through the door on his right that led into the main house. He found himself in a dining room, and his candle revealed a library through the open door straight ahead. The library connected to the parlor, where he had sipped coffee with the Lalauries, the room where Elise had come running in with blood dripping from her finger.

Philippe knew that the stairway to the attic was around the corner in the foyer. He crept to the door that led to the staircase.

The door was locked. Philippe began to try his keys. The first key didn't fit. Neither did the second. As he was about to try the third and last of his keys, he heard the sound of footsteps.

He blew out his candle and retreated into the parlor. Philippe's heart pounded as he felt his way along the wall. He reached the tall, thick curtains that covered a window and slipped behind them. Had anyone been walking down Royal Street, he or she would have seen a man in a white suit standing statue-like between the curtain and the window.

Philippe could hear the footsteps coming from the library. Bastien entered the parlor carrying a lantern. The flame revealed his face with the flickering shadows of a phantom from beyond the grave. Philippe heard him creep to the door leading to the foyer and sniff the air. He watched Bastein spin around and move step by step across the parlor. With one sudden motion, Bastien yanked back the curtains covering the window next to the one where Philippe was hiding.

A brass latch dug deep into the arch of Philippe's boot, but he dared not move his foot. He could tell that his hands were shaking and thought that the sound of his heart must be audible. *More than audible, it must sound like a drum in Congo Square.*

Bastien must have heard a noise. He stepped back, moved to the next window, and tore open the curtains.

The latch was unlocked; the open window leaned toward the street. No one was there, but Philippe worried that Bastien might recognize him as he escaped down Royal Street.

The confessional at the back of the cathedral consisted of a simple wooden panel with a screen. Father Blanc was sitting on one side; Philippe knelt on the other, a white rosary dangling from his hands.

"Well, thank God you were able to escape," the priest's hushed voice said to Philippe. "That was a foolish risk to take. For what? A feeling? You need to be thinking about getting into heaven, not getting into some attic."

"I know it was foolish, but I feel I need to get up there," whispered Philippe.

"To heaven or the attic?" asked Father Blanc. "Philippe, I've seen you comforting people with Marie Laveau at the cemetery. You recognized the Shepherd's passion on the back of a slave. Keep learning to see his face in the marginalized and those who suffer."

"Yes, Father."

"Help your brother care for that girl, and pray that God will reveal what needs to be uncovered in his own time. Still have your mother's rosary? For your penance, say five decades."

Philippe realized that Father Blanc was right. His responsibility now was to Elise. Even if he had found something in the attic, how would he have explained being there to the sheriff?

"Keep learning to see his face in the marginalized and those who suffer."

That was what he had been trying to avoid. *I'll want to protect them, and I'll fail. But Father Blanc is right. I should at least try.*

He continued to comfort those who lost loved ones to the fever and soon began to accompany Marie when she visited the prison after morning Mass. To his surprise, Dr. Miller, the Methodist minister, was already well-known to the prison guards. For years, Philippe had believed that the Protestants, in their eagerness to reform the Church, had thrown the baby out with the holy water.

Now he began to think that this Methodist was far more Christian than he had ever been. It also impressed him that Dr. Miller had learned to speak French. Most Americans refused to even say *"bonjour."* Miller explained that he wanted to visit France someday.

It was after one of those morning visits to the Cabildo that Philippe learned it was Marie who had sent Elise to the cathedral the day she escaped.

I should have figured that out sooner. Of course, the girl would run to Marie's cottage first. It was right there by Congo Square. No wonder Marie wasn't surprised when I said I had sent someone to her shack.

"Pay attention to Marie Laveau," Guy had told him. "She's a wise owl who chooses all of her words with great care."

She was wise enough to know that the sheriff might look for a runaway in the cottage of the voodoo queen, but probably not in the room of a reclusive bookworm. Wise enough to know that changing the color of the girl's tignon might allow her to run unrecognized as far as the cathedral.

Philippe worried whether anybody would notice how often he now headed out toward the bayou. He thought about the picnics at Marie's shack with Elise, Guy, and Brigitte. He remembered how Brigitte had made flash cards with the alphabet and taken them to Elise, and the rainy day he found Elise writing each of those letters on the scraps of paper he had taken to the shack. In no time, he was bringing her children's books.

Each time he visited her, he wanted to question her about the Lalauries, but Brigitte and Marie kept saying all that would accomplish would be to bring back painful memories. "Just love her and let her go on with her life," Brigitte would say.

Just love her. How do you know love? Philippe liked being able to discuss these matters with Father Blanc.

"When you embrace somebody, it might be love, it might be lust," the priest told him. "When you embrace their pain, take it upon yourself as your own, that's love. That's the kind of love God gives to us."

Philippe was not about to inflict any more pain on Elise. He resolved to let go of his desire to ask her about that attic. It was a resolution that he was able to keep until Good Friday, the day he passed the Lalaurie mansion and thought he heard someone inside, someone weeping.

Chapter 7

Easter Week

The sun's radiance beamed through the Spanish moss, inspiring every songbird in the swamp. Elise watched from the shack as Brigitte sniffed the scent of rain lilies in her vase and walked toward the shack with Guy and Philippe.

Guy shifted the heavy basket of food in his arms and broke the silence. "Easter Mass was beautiful," he said, as a nearby blue heron took flight.

"Yes," Brigitte agreed. "Father Blanc's sermon about the Resurrection filled me with hope."

"I suspect he'll be our next bishop," announced Philippe. "At least, that's the rumor that is spreading through the cathedral."

"You going to wait till after dinner to question her?" asked Guy.

"Question me about what?" Elise asked as she climbed down from her spy post in the shack.

"Well, to begin, ask you if you know that it's Easter," Philippe said, as Brigitte handed her the vase of lilies.

Elise beamed with excitement when she saw the Easter feast the Bertrands were unloading from their baskets. The picnic, watching egrets roost on the knees of the cypress, and listening to Guy and Philippe tell stories about growing up on a vineyard in France filled the entire afternoon. It was an Easter Sunday unlike any that Elise had ever known.

The sun was low in the sky when Philippe poked the embers of the little fire and told Elise that they needed to talk. Guy and Brigitte strolled down the path to give them some privacy.

"Elise, you're safe out here, but what about the other slaves at the Lalaurie house?" Philippe began. "I'm worried about them, too. I've waited long enough. It's time to tell me what goes on in that house. No need to be afraid."

Elise turned her head away. "Please," she said, "I ain't afraid of nothin'… Grand-Mère Arnante made me promise."

"Yes, well then think about Grand-Mère for a minute. What if your silence allows something bad to happen to her? Evil depends on silence, you know."

"Evil?" Elise repeated.

"Evil," said Philippe. "I believe that whatever is happening in that house involves personal, diabolical evil. So, tell me, what's in that attic?"

"Me and Bastien, we saw the whole city," Elise said, "but I was never allowed in most of the house. I only seen the attic once."

Philippe appeared determined now. "Elise, lives may be at stake. I need to know. What did you see in that attic?"

Elise lifted the rosary that hung around her neck and gazed at it in silence for a long time before she answered. "Strange things…and dead people."

"Dead people?" repeated Philippe.

"We heard noises sometimes," said Elise. "I figured people were up there… black people from Dominique. It was the food."

"The food?" Philippe asked.

"Servants ate in the courtyard, but at night Bruno would get buckets of gruel from Grand-Mère Arnante and head for the stairs. Grand-Mère Arnante would cry sometimes. 'Those poor souls,' she would say."

Philippe jumped up from where he had been sitting. "Grand-Mère Arnante!" he shouted. "That's the answer. Elise, do you still have the dress you wore when you came here?"

It was late when Philippe returned to his house with Guy. He set down a brown pouch, then lit a candle and placed it on his table next to the jug. He was glad to have the lemonade. It wasn't a hot night, but his throat was dry anyway. *Nerves.* He paced back and forth in front of his books, walked back to the table where Guy was sitting, and poured another glass of lemonade.

"You can't take this to the sheriff," said Guy. "He'd be required to apprehend any runaway slave."

"We'll get Dubois to look in the attic for himself," said Philippe. "Have you ever been up there?"

"No," said Guy. "I inspected the second floor when the fire contract was signed; that's creepy enough. It's full of sliding panels and secret passages."

"We just need to get Dubois to that house," said Philippe.

"Dubois will be at the Lalauries' on Thursday night. Delphine is having her Spring Ball. Brigitte and I are invited," said Guy.

"I don't want Brigitte involved," said Philippe. "But make sure Dubois is coming, and tell him Grand-Mère Arnante will give him enough information to warrant an investigation."

"Arnante doesn't even know you. What makes you think you can get her to talk to the sheriff?"

Philippe pulled a leather pouch out from under the table, reached inside it, and pulled out Elise's gingham dress.

"I need to ask Marie when Delphine is having her hair done for that ball," said Philippe.

It was April 10, and Delphine was furious. The woman whose coif was forever trimmed with great care and who always wore the latest in Parisian fashion now looked as if she had spent the day in a slaughterhouse. Louis stood next to her wearing a lab coat covered with blood.

"Watch where you step," he warned.

"Not only was that a complete failure, his innards are all over the floor now!" yelled Delphine. "Worse yet, I missed my appointment with Marie. My hair will look hideous tonight."

"Maybe you could go now," Louis suggested.

"There are too many up here," Delphine said, looking around the attic. "We have to secure them so that nobody hears anything during the ball."

"The usual place?" asked Louis.

"What choice do we have?" asked Delphine.

Grand-Mère Arnante was alone in the kitchen, shelling peas. With a slow, cautious motion, a handsome young man in a white suite opened the door from the courtyard, stepped into the kitchen, and put his finger to his lips. The sight of the man startled and confused the old cook. She didn't say a word, but backed away as far as her chain would allow.

"I'm Philippe Bertrand, the sacristan at the cathedral," the stranger whispered as he held up Elise's gingham dress.

Arnante stared at it and began to cry. "Elise," she whispered, "is she…?"

"She's safe," Philippe said. "You're all going to be safe. But I need your help. At exactly seven thirty tonight, I will bring the sheriff to this kitchen. Once I convince him to look in the attic, you'll be safe."

Grand-Mère tried to back away farther, but her chain wouldn't permit it. She shook her head.

"I need you to tell him about the buckets of gruel Bruno used to get. That's all. You don't have to say anything else. I promise you, this will save everybody. Can you do that? For Elise?"

Grand-Mère Arnante hesitated. She looked at the dress again before she whispered, "I'll do it."

Arnante picked up some firewood for the oven, and Philippe set the dress on the table in order to help her. He placed a log in the oven and kissed the old woman on the cheek.

"Someone's coming," she whispered.

The sound of footsteps from the main house grew louder as Philippe dashed out the courtyard door. Bastien walked into the kitchen, stared at the table, and picked up the dress. "They gonna kill you, old woman," he said, holding the dress. "They gonna kill you real slow. Oh, what they gonna do to you."

Moments later, Bastien was in the attic, handing the dress to Delphine, while Louis, lab coat covered with blood, stood by in silence.

"Did you ask her?" questioned Delphine.

"She says she found it," said Bastien, "but I heard the door close. She was talking with someone. Sounded like that churchman from the cathedral. Should I unchain her and bring her up?"

"I need her for tonight's ball. We'll deal with her after the guests leave," said Delphine.

Eugene Dubois stepped into his favorite brasserie on Rue Royal just northeast of Saint Louis. If he was going to confront Delphine Lalaurie again, he thought he should brace himself ahead of time with some whiskey and maybe a bite of food.

Guy Bertrand had come to him claiming that his brother would produce a witness who would give him probable cause for an investigation into the illegal importation of slaves from the Caribbean. For the past twenty-six years, it had been against the law to bring slaves into the United States, but Dubois knew it still took place. Delphine's last husband had been involved with the ships that unloaded "black ivory" late at night. There was no doubt about that. But Delphine was married to Louis now, and he didn't appear to be the type.

If anybody knows about this business, it's the men who drink at that house on Bourbon Street, the one with the parrot behind the bar. It's right down the street from Guy's fire station. Maybe he heard someone there talking about the old days. On the other hand, if Guy wanted to drink, why not go to the bar right below his apartment?

Dubois remembered seeing Delphine's coachman standing behind that Bourbon Street bar a few times. *Maybe he was brokering the traffic. No, that didn't make sense. Or did it? No, I doubt the Bertrand brothers will be able to produce as much evidence as Guy claimed.*

As a precaution, he ordered two of his deputies to stay near the Lalaurie mansion tonight, but to stay out of sight. The deputies wore uniforms, and the sheriff did not want to upset the most powerful members of the French Creole community without cause.

Dubois wore his most formal garb, which in his case meant a tie without food stains and a clean shirt. After a drink and a bite of some pastries that the establishment had left over from this morning, Dubois put on his hat and headed for the chestnut mare hitched to the post outside. He was just three steps onto the street when he heard the cussing and commotion. It was coming from the little courtyard next door. The sheriff peeked into the dark walkway and saw two drunken keelboatmen brandishing enormous knives.

"All right, you two. Enough!" yelled Dubois as he stepped into the courtyard.

Before he could do anything else, the louder of the two plunged his knife into the other one's chest. The wounded man moaned, and fell to the ground. His wound sucked air and spurted blood for a moment before he died. Dubois pulled his pistol and put it to the head of the man who was still standing.

"Drop the knife, or I'll turn your brain into gumbo," said Dubois.

Once the knife hit the ground, Dubois kicked it aside, took out a set of shackles from his belt, cuffed the culprit, and led him out onto Rue Royale. He fastened the shackles to a rope tied to the horn of his horse's saddle.

"Americans! Buckskinned heathens," he said, spitting a plug of tobacco into a pool of horse piss on the street. "I'm supposed to be at the first party since Carnival, and now I have to deal with you."

The music was soft enough that Philippe and Guy could discern bits and pieces of a dozen conversations even as they walked across the ballroom.

Delphine was scurrying about seeing to the needs of her guests, each of whom competed to display the most chic spring fashion. Her own dress was black embroidered silk with white lace sleeves. A golden cord around her neck suspended her blue velvet bag. She glowed like the chandeliers that hung from the gilded ceiling above her head.

Dr. Miller, clerical collar about his neck and tall lemonade in his hand, strolled past the mahogany-framed occasional chairs that had been placed with care between the candles on the wall.

"Dr. Miller," Philippe said, "I see Methodist ministers are part of this crowd."

"And now they are letting in Catholic sacristans," said Miller as he passed Philippe and Guy.

Louis appeared behind them as if he had materialized from nowhere. Philippe was startled when the voice over his shoulder said, "Figured you'd know him. An American, but his preaching is very un-American. All his talk about social justice. Gonna lead to a slave revolt like Turner in Virginia. You just read books, right? No harm in that."

Philippe spotted Augustine Macarty speaking with Henri Bonnet and used it as an excuse to break away from Louis.

"Ah, there's M'sieur Macarty. I should say hello," said Philippe as he stepped away.

"He's keeping an eye on us," warned Guy as they moved toward Macarty.

"Watching us like a hawk," said Philippe. "Dubois should be here by now, but I don't see him."

Philippe began to fiddle with his collar as he and Guy walked over and stood behind Augustine.

"I see the Senate voted to censure Old Hickory over this bank thing. Y'all know he headquartered at our plantation during the war," boasted Augustine.

"Jackson did the right thing," said Henri. "The bank only serves the interests of the Eastern elite."

"Fascinating topic, the interests of the elite," Philippe said.

Augustine leaned on his cane and shifted his stance to see who was speaking. "Gentlemen, good to see y'all," he said. "We were discussing the president. Have you been following the story in the newspapers?"

"I read the French section of the *Bee* on occasion, but I much prefer to read books," said Philippe.

"Any authors you particularly recommend?" asked Augustine.

"I just started a book by a woman named Mary Shelley," said Philippe.

The music stopped.

"Here we are at a party, with real live people, and you talk about reading books," Guy said to his brother.

"Follow me, gentlemen," said Henri. "The judge is going to teach us a new game he learned on the riverboats. It's called *poque*."

"No, thanks. Have you seen Sheriff Dubois?" Philippe asked.

"Not tonight," said Henri as he headed toward a door behind and to the left of the orchestra.

Philippe and Guy scanned the ballroom once more for Dubois, and then decided to return to the foyer.

"I'm worried," Philippe said. "I told Arnante seven thirty. It's well past eight. Let's wait for him outside."

"Fine," said Guy before sniffing the air and looking outside the door. "Wait. Do you smell smoke?"

Within thirty seconds, Guy's experience as a firefighter enabled him to trace the source of the smoke. It was coming from above and behind the house.

"The kitchen," said Guy.

They ran onto Rue Royale, rounded the corner onto Hospital Street, and hurried past four ballroom windows and two more that allowed them to look into a parlor where Judge Canonge was playing cards. Philippe peered into one of those windows to see if Dubois was in the card game. He wasn't.

Stepping into the courtyard, they saw that the kitchen level of the annex was on fire. They hurried across the courtyard and opened the kitchen door.

The heat of the inferno struck Philippe's face with a painful blast. Hellish flames engulfed Grand-Mère Arnante's entire body. Madison was trying to protect his face with one arm while swinging a blanket with the other. His attempts to smother the flames from the old woman's dress were futile. She collapsed to the floor, still burning. Philippe struggled to pull Madison back toward the door.

"It's too late," Philippe told Madison. "She's gone. What happened here?"

Madison caught his breath. "Grand-Mère Arnante started it," he said.

"She's chained to the floor!" said Guy.

"I know, m'sieu," Madison said. "She said she wanted to die."

"Nobody wants to die like that!" said Philippe. "To be burned alive? My god!"

"She kept crying, 'They ain't comin', they ain't comin'.' Next thing she be pourin' grease all over and there's fire everywhere," said Madison.

The blaze was spreading toward the door. Flaming debris began to fall from the ceiling.

"Come on!" yelled Guy. "We have to get out of here. Servants' quarters are over the kitchen. I'll head up there."

L'immortalité

"I'll start evacuating the ballroom," said Philippe.

Guy addressed Madison. "Your name?" he asked.

"Madison, m'sieu."

"Madison, my hook-and-ladder company is two blocks down. Take a left on Saint Philip. Run and get my brigade."

More debris fell from the ceiling as the three men backed out of the doorway into the courtyard. Guy started up the outer staircase that led to the slave quarters, looking back just long enough to yell one word: "Hurry!"

Music played, and the dance floor was crowded with couples as Philippe ran into the ballroom and made his way over to the orchestra.

"Quiet, please!" he hollered.

The music stopped, but the murmuring of the crowd grew louder, and an angry-looking Delphine Lalaurie dashed over to find out what was happening. Seconds later, the crowd began to quiet down and focus on Philippe.

"A fire has broken out in the annex," Philippe said in a cool, unruffled, but strong voice. "Please stay calm, but leave the house at once."

"Pick up your things and set up on the street," Delphine told the musicians. "There is no need to end this party over a little kitchen fire. I won't have it."

Delphine maintained her composure but called out to her guests in her loudest voice, "We are simply moving the party out to Rue Royale as a precaution. Bring your drinks, just changing locations."

"Your footman has gone to get the fire company," Philippe told Delphine. "There is nothing left of the kitchen. We couldn't save the cook."

Delphine's only response was to shrug and walk away. She showed emotion only when smoke began to drift into the ballroom.

"My furniture!" cried Delphine. "My imported furniture and paintings! For god's sake, save the furniture!"

Philippe was enraged. "Madame!" he hollered. "I said Grand-Mère Arnante is dead."

The expression on Madame Lalaurie's face transformed into something more hideous than Philippe had ever seen before, something diabolical. Her eyes were no longer the soft, flirtatious coffee-brown lanterns that fluttered when she first invited him for coffee. Looking into them now, Philippe saw something altogether alien.

"My runaway you've been harboring," she sneered, "did you manage to save that dress you left in my kitchen?" Delphine pressed her face close to Philippe's. "Blame yourself, you pious bastard."

Delphine spun on her heels and walked away. Around the ballroom, men were picking up chairs and small tables. Delphine led them to the street. Philippe could see the orchestra already heading out the door with their instruments and music stands. He followed them.

"This way, gentlemen, follow me," Delphine called out.

On Royal Street, the flickering light from the annex fire glowed in the sky from behind the house. Men were placing chairs in the street, and the orchestra was setting up to play. Smoke drifted like phantoms through the air, leaving behind the acrid odor of something from hell. Women in silk gowns sipped their drinks, as if partying during a fire were a normal routine in the Vieux Carré. More furniture and paintings emerged from the house in the arms of French Creole gentlemen being directed by their hostess. The music started up again, but now without a piano.

"Gentlemen, please be sure to get all the paintings from the parlors," Delphine called out.

Only Philippe and Dr. Miller were ignoring her orders. Dubois arrived on horseback just as Judge Canonge was passing through the entrance portal with a large vase in his hands.

"What's going on?" Dubois asked as he dismounted his mare. "Is everyone safe?"

"Where the hell have you been?" Philippe yelled at the sheriff. "The woman Guy told you about is dead."

Dr. Miller interrupted. "Where are all the servants?"

"Only a few in the servants' quarters," Guy called out as he came around the corner.

"Madame Lalaurie, where are the rest of the servants?" Philippe demanded.

"Never mind them, save my Oriental carpets," said Delphine as she pointed at Philippe and added, "and, Sheriff, that man is a thief."

"Damn you!" Philippe yelled at Delphine. "Where are the rest of the slaves?"

"Yes, where are the servants?" Judge Canonge joined in.

Dubois seemed oblivious to their yelling. His eyes were focused on Madison, the arriving firefighters, and his deputies, who had finally noticed all the commotion on Royal Street.

Philippe ran back into the house. There, in the foyer, Louis Lalaurie was standing guard in front of the locked door that led to the staircase. He clutched a set of keys in his hand.

Philippe could hear frantic pounding coming from the other side of the door. "The stairway!" he exclaimed. "Open that door at once."

"No," said Louis. Considering the frantic sounds coming from behind the door, the calmness of his voice was eerie. "I don't want anybody tampering with my experiments. Stay away."

Philippe noticed smoke seeping out from a crack above the door. The heavy door muted the sound of coughing and the relentless pounding, but it was clear that somebody was desperate to get out.

"My God, man, there are human beings in there," said Philippe as he tried to reach for the keys. Louis pulled away. "Hand over those…"

Grabbing Louis by the arm, Philippe began to twist. The sudden move brought Louis to his knees, but only for a moment. Louis stood and pulled a candlestick from the desk behind him. The tiny flame at the top of the beeswax candle vanished as the candlestick swung through the air toward Philippe's head.

Philippe's left arm blocked the intended blow. He countered with a hard punch to the doctor's jaw, and kicked Louis in the groin. The keys fell to the black-and-white checkered floor. Reaching down, Philippe grasped the doctor by the collar and hurled him out the front door toward Royal Street.

"I'll kill you," snarled Louis, looking up from the exterior marble tiles that lined the floor of the portal outside the mansion's black threshold.

Philippe picked up the keys and fumbled with one of them. The pounding on the door grew more intense. The first key did not fit, but in seconds that felt more like hours, Philippe was able to open the door with the next key on the ring. Smoke poured out the open door as eight naked slaves, each bent over in fits of coughing, staggered to freedom.

Madison appeared in the foyer. Philippe guided the slaves across the foyer to the front door, leaned out, and shouted, "I need a few brave men! The smoke's heavy, and it sounds like more servants are upstairs!"

A handful of slaves ran into the foyer. Philippe and Madison took candles from the desk and led them through the doorway and up the stairs. Philippe pulled a white rosary from his pocket as they made their way up the dark, smoky staircase. They stopped at the second-floor landing. It was quiet at that level, but Philippe thought he heard noises above him in the attic.

The door at the top of the stairs was barred from the outside. Philippe removed the wooden bar and tried the door. It was locked. In less than a minute, he determined that none of the keys on the ring he had taken from Lalaurie would open the lock. The slaves began to batter the door with the wooden bar. Philippe didn't know if they would be able to break through.

Chapter 8

Breakthrough

A s the slaves in front of him battered the door, Philippe didn't know that Father Blanc was kneeling for vespers inside the dark cathedral. He didn't know that Marie was busy lighting candles in her cottage on Saint Ann Street. He didn't know that a set of white beads was moving through Elise's fingers as she watched the stars glimmer over the bayou. It's certain that he didn't know that the Lalauries' attic was about to reveal a secret that would change everything.

He had wanted to get into that attic for months, and now, with one final heave of the wooden bar, one final thrust, the door sprung open.

"Cleopas!" screamed one of the slaves, recognizing the face.

Philippe stepped around him and held out his candle. Its light reflected off the face of a severed head, wires wrapped crown-like around its forehead. Impaled on a spike, the face of the Haitian man once known as Cleopas was less than two feet from Philippe's own. Philippe fell to his knees in shock, dropping his mother's rosary and watching it disappear through a crack in the cypress-planked floor.

"My Lord!" cried Philippe, resting his hand on the floor as nausea began to make him feel like the room was spinning.

"To see his face in the marginalized and those who suffer."

He lifted his hand from the wet, sticky floor. Semi-congealed blood covered his fingers. He stared back up at the severed head. Eyes half open, tongue protruding, the head of Cleopas did not resemble Marie's idealized painting of the Baptist. No, this was far more brutal, far too real. There, thought Philippe, were eyes that once cried for their mother. A tongue that once pleaded for mercy. Ears that had listened to the drums in Congo Square. Philippe began to vomit.

Only then did he notice the swarms of flies that filled the room.

"Get Sheriff Dubois!" Philippe called to the slaves behind him. "Tell him to get up here at once."

Madison and the other slaves stood frozen in horror for a moment, and then ran down the stairs to find Dubois. Philippe noticed a small gable window at floor level near the stairs. He reached over and opened the shutters in hope that some of the smoke would flow from the attic.

Once able to stand again, Philippe held out his candle, and then almost dropped it as he screamed and jumped, startled by the hand that touched his shoulder. Reeling around, he saw that the hand belonged to a girl chained to the wall, her mouth sewn shut. The darkness obscured her mangled limbs at first, but Philippe's candle soon revealed what had been done to her.

"And that fellow across the room owns a circus."

Somehow, the girl was still clinging to life. Philippe tried to remove her chains as the reality of what had happened to her…and why…began to sink in.

See the Amazing Crab Girl.

Philippe began unfastening the chains from the wall. "You're safe now; we'll get you out of here," he tried to say. Both his nausea and the thick smoke made it difficult to speak.

Dubois, Guy, and Madison ran into the laboratory carrying lanterns. Dubois stopped when the gruesome scene appeared before him.

"Mother of God!"

"Cut her loose," Philippe said, letting go of the girl's chains and heading toward the back of the attic. "Sounds like someone else is alive back there."

Madison went to work trying to loosen the chains that secured the girl to the wall while Dubois and Guy followed Philippe. As they made their way through the dark, smoky attic, their lanterns began to reveal dead bodies strapped to makeshift operating tables.

"This one is dead," said Guy. "My God! His eyes have been plucked out."

Dubois touched the forehead of the body. He lifted and dropped its arm. "So have the fingernails. This one has been dead for a while, but his death must have been slow and painful."

Philippe heard a coughing sound, but it was too dark to see where it had come from. They passed another body, then another and another. Dubois held his lantern over yet another victim.

"Can't even tell if this was a man or a woman," he said.

Philippe took five more steps, and recoiled. In the darkness, he had come face-to-face with a dead slave who was hanging by his neck from a chain and a heavy iron spiked collar.

"Hurry," yelled Guy. "Here in the corner, in the cage, another slave and she's alive."

"She can't walk," said Dubois. "Guy, go down and have Dr. Miller cut the canvas from one of Delphine's damned paintings. We'll use it as a litter. I have to find Lalaurie."

Guy and Dubois headed to the stairs. Philippe went back to help Madison with the girl, who was now unchained from the wall.

Philippe and Madison carried the girl down the stairs. When they got to the second-floor landing, they were startled by a sliding panel that opened behind them. Delphine stepped out from a passage behind the panel and held a gun to the back of Philippe's head.

"Put her down," Delphine ordered.

The two men placed the girl on the floor.

"You pious, meddling ass," Delphine hissed at Philippe. "You've ruined me. Now you are going to die for it."

Madison spun around and grabbed Delphine's arm. *Bam!* The gun fired. At once, the crimson tint of blood covered Madison's shirt. He slumped and tumbled headlong down the staircase. Philippe lurched forward trying to catch him.

A second gunshot echoed through the stairwell. Philippe realized it had missed him and saw Delphine retreat into the sliding panel before she disappeared into the darkness. He picked up the girl and struggled to carry her down to the foyer, praying that Delphine would not reappear.

Outside on Royal Street, a firefighter, his face covered with soot, began reporting to Guy. The orchestra played, and the party continued. Firefighters set down their axes and buckets and tried to remain civil as they carried Arnante's charred body out to the street.

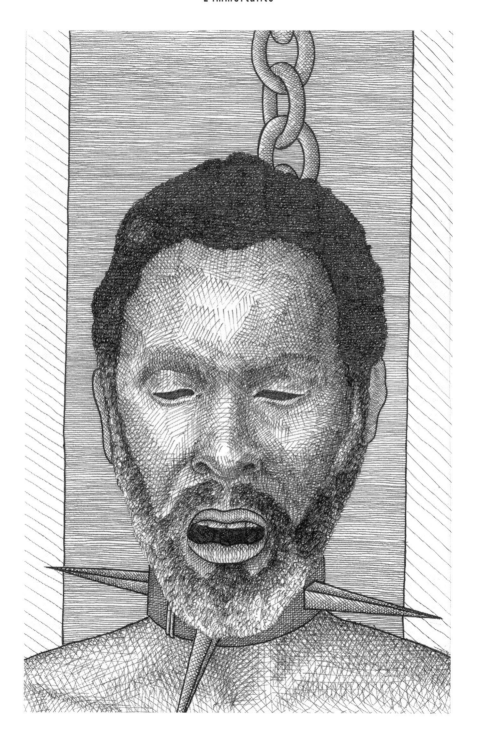

"That poor woman," Guy said.

"How desperate does a person have to be before they're willing to die that way?" the fireman wondered.

"Until a few minutes ago, I could not have imagined it," said Guy.

"Where the hell is Louis?" Dubois yelled as he walked toward Guy. "You," he shouted to one of his deputies, "go check the courtyard!"

The doorman approached with a silver tray holding several shot glasses of liquor.

"What the hell is that?" the sheriff asked.

"Bourbon, m'sieu," said the doorman.

Dubois picked up a shot glass, slugged down the bourbon in one gulp, and slammed the glass back onto the tray.

"Have you seen the Lalauries?" he asked.

"Dr. Lalaurie was yelling at Judge Canonge to mind his own business right after we first came outside, but I haven't seen him since," the doorman told him.

"Get rid of those damn drinks," said Dubois. "Start sending these people home."

Guy looked up to see one of the firefighters carrying Delphine's bullwhip. He set it across a tall china vase that Judge Canonge had placed in the street.

"I saw the doctor go back into the house a while ago. Thought he was in the attic with you," the firefighter told Guy.

"Damn!" said Dubois.

One of the deputies approached leading a group of slaves, many of whom appeared to be starving.

"Take the slaves to the Cabildo. Keep them safe, and give them some food," the sheriff told his deputy. "If you see any more of our men, send them this way."

The deputy pointed to the front door of the mansion. Philippe was carrying the slave girl out of the house. He set her on the ground and stood there panting, hands on his knees. The deputy and one of the firefighters ran over to help the girl.

Guy saw his brother and began to applaud. The firefighters joined in the applause.

"Philippe, what you did was heroic," said Guy.

Philippe staggered over to the china vase, still out of breath.

"Madison's dead," he told his brother.

"What?"

"Delphine shot him. He gave his life for mine. It's the slaves who are the heroes tonight," said Philippe.

"I want you to leave here now. I don't know where Louis is. Who knows what he will do if he sees you. Go home. That's an order," Dubois told Philippe. Guy noticed the sheriff's eyes begin to scan the crowd.

If it was danger the sheriff sensed, his instinct was right. Less than five seconds later, a gunshot rang out, and the china vase next to Philippe shattered to bits. Guy, the doorman, Dubois, and two of the firefighters all took cover behind various pieces of furniture that had been moved into the street. Only Philippe remained standing.

One of the firefighters pointed to the second floor. "There!" he cried.

"Philippe, get out of here now!" Dubois shouted.

Guy looked down and saw the bullwhip resting on top of the china shards that, moments ago, had been an expensive vase. He watched as Philippe picked up the whip and stared at it.

"Philippe, I'm serious," said the sheriff. "Leave. It's not safe for you to be here right now. Go! Go!"

Guy stood and put his arm around his brother. Philippe began to walk with Guy, bullwhip in hand. They headed down Royal Street toward Saint Philip and made it to Guy's apartment before the real trouble began.

Despite all the smoke, the fire did not spread much beyond the annex that held the kitchen and slave quarters. Once the rescued slaves arrived at the Cabildo, however, the news of their treatment and condition spread from the river to Rampart Street, and from the mansion to Canal Street, in no time. Dubois had sent some of the instruments of torture found in the attic to the Cabildo, as well. His intent was to place his evidence in safekeeping.

Instead, his deputies put the spiked collars, drills, and saws caked with blood on display in the prison yard.

The first to notice the assortment of tools that Louis Lalaurie used to torment his slaves was a group of rowdy Cajun fishermen. They had been waiting outside the Cabildo hoping to bail out somebody they called Garçon de Gator.

Garçon de Gator was beyond drunk and had been arrested for hitting a deputy.

The drunken man had an explanation. He claimed the deputy was a werewolf who was chasing him because he hadn't fasted during Lent. After the desk sergeant told them to come back in the morning, the Cajuns decided to spend the night in Pirates Alley.

"Dem things is horrible," said one of the fishermen as one of the deputies put a set of spiked collars on a table inside the Cabildo gate.

"Look at the poor souls they were used on," said the deputy, pointing to the line of emaciated slaves being carried into the yard.

A moment ago, the Cajuns had been laughing and smashing hard-boiled eggs together, an Easter game their great grandfathers had brought from Acadia. Now, the sight of the Lalaurie slaves, their horrifying condition, and the deputy's report of the discoveries on Royal Street transformed their joviality into anger. Garçon de Gator would have to wait until morning. It was time to dish out some Cajun justice.

What began as a few fishermen with too much whiskey under their belts grew larger, louder, and uglier as it moved down Royal Street toward the mansion. "Get down with us to dat mansion," the Cajuns called out, telling everyone they met what they had seen.

By the time Guy's firefighters arrived back at their station, the angry mob forming in front of the Lalaurie mansion numbered well over a hundred men and women.

Dubois knew he couldn't reason with them. A few in the throng carried torches, and one man was already tying a rope into a noose. It was impossible to take in everything they were shouting, but the sheriff was able to make out fragments of sentences.

"Mutilating them," someone said.

"Right here in the Vieux Carré," said another. "Why aren't they under arrest?"

When the first brick was hurled into a tall ballroom window, Dubois knew that he and his two deputies could do nothing to prevent what he was sure would soon become a lynching.

Then, without warning, the carriage gate crashed open with the thunderous sound of a cannon. Wheels scraped against the narrow brick arch as the Lalaurie carriage burst through at breakneck speed. Bastien steered the four black steeds straight into the crowd. The mob began to dive and jump to avoid being trampled by the horses.

Delphine and Louis ducked down inside the carriage as Dubois tried to pull Bastien from the driver's box. Bastien lashed out at him with his whip. The lead horses reared, eyes peeled back, nostrils wide.

"Stop them! They're getting away," one man yelled out.

"Shoot the horses!" someone screamed.

Dubois pulled his pistol and fired at the carriage as it fled, rattling and racing toward the Tremé. A few men ran after it until it disappeared down Hospital Street.

Once the Lalauries' carriage was out of sight, the mob surged toward the mansion and began looting. Within minutes, a group of men had pushed a piano from Delphine's sewing parlor through the wrought iron railing of the second-floor gallery. It crashed onto the street and shattered.

"Sheriff, we can't stop this!" yelled said one of the deputies.

"Go to the barracks and get the army regulars before somebody gets hurt," ordered Dubois as another brick went sailing past his head.

Bastien pulled the reins, and the horses lurched to a stop next to a large tree. It was silent along the bayou that night. Bastien jumped from the box. Delphine and Louis stepped from the carriage, and Bastien retrieved a spade from inside the coach. Delphine pointed to a spot near the tree.

"Right about here, wouldn't you say, Bastien?" she asked.

"Yes, ma'am," said Bastien before rolling up his sleeves and beginning to dig.

"Why did we stop here?" asked Louis. "Who are you digging up?"

"Not who, you old fool, what!" said Delphine. "Your Galvanism cost me everything I had. Everything except what I buried here."

"My work was patriotic," said Louis. "What you did was for sadistic pleasure, nothing else."

"That it was," said Delphine. "More pleasure than I ever got from three husbands! What did you accomplish?"

"I was almost there. Almost beyond Dr. Lefebre in France. And now this," Louis said as his eyes began to fill with tears.

"It's here, *madame*. I found it," Bastien interrupted.

Bastien set the spade aside, got on his knees, and brushed away some mud before straining to pull a heavy bag out of the hole. Louis helped him carry the bag to the coach.

"From the Gulf we can buy passage to New York," said Delphine.

"New York!" exclaimed Bastien. "Oh, thank you, ma'am. In New York, I'll be free. Of course I'd continue—"

Delphine cut him off. "Why, Bastien, my Bastien, we couldn't have escaped without you. You saved us. You don't have to wait to get to New York. I'll set you free tonight."

"Oh, Madame Lalaurie!"

"And as a free man, you deserve to be paid for your efforts. Hand me my purse. It's in the carriage."

Bastien reached into the carriage, retrieved a large purse, and handed it to Delphine. She opened it, looked inside, and with startling swiftness pulled out a pistol. The shot rang out before Bastien even noticed the gun. He stood for a moment, a wound visible between his eyes, then fell to the ground.

"To Mandeville?" asked Louis.

"Yes," answered Delphine. "You can send a power of attorney to Auguste from there."

Delphine hoped that word would arrive in Mandeville that they could return to New Orleans, but if necessary, she had other options.

Louis looked down on Bastien's body. "Let's get out of here," he said.

Delphine wasted no time climbing back into her carriage when she saw a large alligator claw its way out of the swamp. As the Lalauries rode away, the gator hissed, and crawled toward Bastien's body.

A riverboat whistled as it propelled its way up the Mississippi, passing Philippe and Marie as they strolled along the bank. The honking of wild geese concealed the swishing resonance of the boat's paddle wheel. Marie carried Zombie's basket, and Philippe carried Delphine Lalaurie's bullwhip like a trophy. They found a place where the grass was dry and sat.

"So peaceful," said Philippe. "I could stay here forever."

"With all this grime and smoke from the steamboats?" asked Marie.

"Well, it's better than the stench of that cemetery, and it's away from that mansion." Philippe could not shake the horrors of the attic from his mind. "How is that kind of evil even possible?" he asked.

"How is it possible? Fear. Fear," repeated Marie. "People suspected, but they were afraid of being excluded. Afraid it might change things. Fear makes people close their eyes."

Marie pulled Zombie out of his basket and stroked him before she continued.

"I've watched people close their eyes when I showed them this beautiful creature," she said. "See? There is nothing to fear here."

Philippe could hear the geese honking as he looked at the snake. Marie stood, and at once, a large flock of geese sprang up from the swamp grass behind her and took flight. The voodoo queen stretched out her hand and reached down to Philippe.

"The spirits are calling them home," said Marie, her eyes tracking the geese as they began to form a *V* in the sky. "Rise up, Philippe. Don't become like me. Rise up and answer your calling."

Philippe stood and hurled the bullwhip into the river.

"That's what I intend to do," said Philippe with a firmness and resolve that startled Marie. "Excuse me," he said. "I need to find Father Blanc."

A few hours later, Father Blanc and Philippe turned out of Pirates Alley. They were approaching the cathedral's front doors when Philippe cleared his throat and broke the silence.

"Father Antoine, I need a favor."

"We have no bishop, so you want me to write to the seminary," Father Blanc replied with a smile.

"How? How did you know?" asked Philippe.

"Philippe, what did you see in that attic?"

"Bodies."

"No, Philippe," the priest replied, "at last, you saw souls. You felt the power of compassion. How could I be with you every day and not know that?"

"Father, what happened up there was so evil...demonic...and all because of what was not done, what was not said. I have..."

"Accepted your calling, learned to love again," said Father Blanc, finishing Philippe's sentence. "Of course, I will write, and of course, you will be accepted."

Father Blanc put his arm around Philippe's shoulder, gave him a gentle squeeze, and disappeared into the cathedral. Marie Laveau passed him as she exited the church.

"Marie, I have news," said Philippe when he saw her. "I'm going back to the seminary."

"Oh, Philippe, that's wonderful. And you didn't believe in my voodoo. I have news, too. I've been asking the spirits to guide me in making a decision, and I can't wait to tell you what I've decided to do. I'm bringing Elise to Rue Saint Anne to live with me. She can't stay out in that swamp forever."

Philippe agreed with Marie's decision. *It's safe now. The Lalauries are gone.*

"I'll say she's a daughter who has been away, change her name to Marie, teach her a craft," said Marie.

It would work, Philippe thought. He had noticed that Elise resembled Marie in many ways, and knowing Marie, somehow sealed and notarized papers would appear both at her house and in the records at the Cabildo to prove that she had given birth to the girl. "Official" records often appeared and disappeared in New Orleans. That was one trick Philippe believed Marie Laveau's voodoo could accomplish.

Philippe wanted to stay and talk, but something was waiting for him inside the cathedral, something he needed to do.

Two Maries. I wonder if New Orleans is ready for that!

A line was beginning to form leading into the alley. The *New Orleans Bee* was on the streets, and those in line all had a copy of the paper in their hands. Sheriff Dubois was amazed at how many people had come after reading about the fire and the condition of the slaves. Now they waited in line just to peer into the courtyard and see the evidence for themselves. Dubois had not read the article yet, so he asked one of the Irish laborers who was in line to see his copy. The editor's words summed up what Dubois had already come to believe.

We cannot but regard the manner in which these atrocities have been brought to light as an especial interposition of heaven.

Dubois handed the paper back to the Irishman and stepped into the side door of the cathedral. A wooden coffin rested in the center aisle. Philippe was placing a printed placard on top of it, reading: *Madison, the compassionate servant.*

Philippe began arranging some flowers around the coffin before he noticed the sheriff. "Heard you're boarding up the Lalaurie house," he said.

"For a while I wondered if that house was haunted," said Dubois. "I kept hearing this knocking." Dubois demonstrated what he meant by rapping his fist three times on the lid of the coffin.

"Well, I suppose life after death is the premise behind all hauntings," said Philippe. "I once thought I heard a voice singing the Kyrie outside my window at night. Some of the priests at the cathedral told me it was the ghost of Père Dagobert and that his singing was not an uncommon occurrence."

"I've heard that singing myself," said Dubois, "but in this case, it wasn't ghosts. I discovered more slaves under the attic floorboards. They were dead by the time we found them."

Philippe stopped arranging flowers around the coffin and made the sign of the cross. "May they rest in peace," he said.

"With Madison," Dubois added. "I curse the day I returned him to that house. He was a compassionate servant."

"As I hope to become," said Philippe.

The firemen covered the best white meat from an alligator tail in lemon juice, paprika, garlic powder, salt, and pepper before dipping it in eggs and flour. It was a man-size midnight snack, but they had put in a hard day's work. As his crew began to sauté the gator steaks in lard, Guy excused himself and headed back out to Saint Philip Street. He had already spent half an hour in the bar below his apartment drinking brandy-milk punch before walking over to the hook-and-ladder company. Prior to that, he had tossed and turned in his bed for over an hour, keeping Brigitte awake with his constant shifting and pillow fluffing.

Guy's mind raced between shadows of Grand-Mère Arnante engulfed in flames, worries about his company's reputation as "the Lalaurie fire crew," concerns for his aging father, and an intensified loathing for the practice of slavery. His thoughts skipped across each of these subjects like a flat rock tossed across Bayou Saint John. That he couldn't focus his thoughts on any one topic for more than a minute only increased his anxiety.

Alcohol was the wrong answer, he told himself. He'd thought some time with the fire crew would take his mind off his concerns, but the odor of the gator meat simmering in the pan exacerbated the nausea brought on by the images in his mind of Grand-Mère Arnante's horrifying death.

Guy headed through the fog toward Pirates Alley. He made it as far as Saint Ann Street before deciding that it would be unreasonable for him to wake his brother at this hour just because *he* couldn't sleep.

He reversed his course and walked back up Royal Street, stopping when he reached the dark, ornate house that had once been home to Judge Francois X. Martin. The doctor who now owned the property claimed that the ghost of Judge Martin could be heard stumbling around the house day and night.

The old judge had gone blind and, according to Marie Laveau, considered his blindness a blessing. Marie said the judge believed that heaven had allowed him to lose his sight in order to teach him the absurdity of using skin color to determine how people would, or could, be treated. Guy had never met the judge. He'd died before Guy arrived in New Orleans. Having spent his youth in a place where color was much less of an issue, Guy shared Judge Martin's belief that the Louisiana social stratification according to various shades of skin color was absurd.

Guy stared at the white pillars of the Martin House for a few minutes, thinking about his life in France and ignoring the bats that circled the streetlamp overhead. Then, instead of turning toward his apartment on Saint Philip Street, he walked two more blocks down Royal and returned to the Lalaurie mansion for the first time since the fire.

Splinters of wood and parts of a keyboard, black keys next to white, were still scattered along Hospital Street where Delphine's piano had landed on the stone pavement. The pungent odor of burned cypress lingered in the air. Guy peered through the open gate into the courtyard. The heat from the fire had caused the bougainvillea to shed many of its papery red bracts onto the flagstones of the terrace. *Like drops of blood*, Guy said to himself. The upright beams that had framed the kitchen were charred. To Guy they resembled the square-scaled black skin of the alligator carcass he had seen earlier that night at the fire hall.

It appeared as if the luminescence of fluorescent green fireflies danced in the air and, for an instant, a sapphire blue light flashed over his head. He blinked his eyes, and it was gone. *I need to get some sleep.*

That's when he saw it. At least he thought he was seeing it. For about fifteen seconds, the transparent specter of Grand-Mère Arnante appeared to float over the balcony of the Lalaurie mansion, gently holding and caressing the phantom body of little Leah.

The phantasm faded into a dark, ashen mist as quickly as it had appeared. Guy ran back to his apartment, wondering with each step down Royal Street if he had actually seen a manifestation from beyond the grave or if the stress of the fire and lack of sleep were combining to bring on some terrifying form of dementia.

Philippe opened the bright yellow door to his apartment on the first knock. He didn't ask Guy why he had missed morning Mass or why he looked so tired. Since childhood, he had known that it was best to wait for his brother to tell him when something was wrong. The two remained silent for several minutes while Guy began to help Philippe sort his books and stack them into crates.

Some of the books Philippe would keep—the *Summa Theologica*, *Zoology of the Southern States*, *French-English Dictionary*—but he planned to give most of them away. One pile on the table, labeled "poetry," was going to Elise. Another group on the floor, fiction, he would give to Guy. A priest at the cathedral had requested any books on philosophy.

"What does the church say will happen to Grand-Mère Arnante?" Guy asked, finally breaking the silence. "I mean, it was a suicide."

Philippe set down the book in his hand and took a deep breath. "One of the things I've learned since I began talking with the prisoners at the Cabildo is that Judge Canonge never issues his sentences without considering what he calls 'mitigating factors,'" he said. "I doubt that our souls are adjudicated by a less understanding judge than Jean Canonge."

"Don't think I'm crazy, but I could swear I saw her ghost last night at the Lalaurie mansion."

"If I said you were crazy, it would be for going to that house in the middle of the night, not for believing in life after death."

"So, you think it might have been real?"

"It seems possible to me that her spirit would have difficulty letting go of all the hurt, the injustice, the anger she must have felt. Yes, it's possible."

"I don't ever want to see someone die like that again. I've been up all night wondering if I should sell the fire company and go back to France."

"Father would be delighted to have you to take over the vineyard, but he is in good health and will send for you if he needs you. For now, don't do anything hasty. You've worked hard to build that company."

"Private fire companies may not have much of a future," said Guy, "and there are some other things I really don't like about living here."

"Slavery?" Philippe asked. The idea of one human being owning another was abhorrent to both brothers. "That doesn't have much of a future either. Even the British are doing away with it."

"That and the disease. The air is clear and fresh in the vineyard, and Brigitte wants to start a family."

"I suppose someone who is about to take a vow of celibacy can't claim to be an expert, but it seems to me that if you want a family, walking around the Vieux Carré all night long might not be the best way to get started. Guy, take your time, get some rest, and trust in prayer. You're young and have plenty of time to discern what's best."

"I know I need some sleep. It's just hard to get that fire out of my mind, and Delphine Lalaurie."

"She'll never walk these streets again," said Philippe.

Guy nodded. "I wonder where she went?"

Chapter 9

France

The empty eye sockets of a hundred human skulls gazed at Louis and Delphine in the flickering firelight. Delphine was roasting a piece of meat on the coals. Louis sat there feeling confused and horrified. He had owned slaves who lived better than this. Delphine had made them fugitives in Louisiana, and now they faced the same fate in France. From a mansion on Royal Street they had been reduced to hiding in the underground ossuary on the south side of Paris, the network of tunnels and ancient stone mines that held the bones of countless dead Parisians.

When they first arrived in France, he assumed that his life would continue in the lavish, comfortable style he had known after marrying Delphine. Her son-in-law had arranged for them to stay at a family member's majestic estate a few miles outside of Paris. In fact, the correspondence from Auguste Delassus had arrived at his cousin's estate only days before Louis and Delphine showed up at the door. What had been known as a mansion in New Orleans could fit inside any one of the three wings of the house that welcomed them in France.

The welcome was short-lived. The unexpected arrival of Dr. Miller from New Orleans changed everything. Louis remembered the indignity of being asked to leave in the middle of the night after the minister told their hosts what had been discovered in the attic of the Lalaurie mansion. A brief stay with his own family didn't work out much better. Delphine insisted on leaving when Louis's father began to mock her obvious insanity.

The gold held out for a few more months, but Delphine was not about to reduce her standard of living, at least of her own accord. She reminded Louis that her first husband had been knighted. She was entitled to be addressed as Lady Delphine Ramón Lalaurie. Some lady! Now even common merchants looked at her tattered clothes with disdain. When the gold ran out, Delphine was the least-equipped person in Paris to attempt to survive on the streets. Unskilled as a pickpocket, unwilling to beg, and married to a man too soft and pudgy to strong-arm anyone, the woman who had once ruled French Creole society in New Orleans decided in her desperation to stab a young prostitute in the back in order to steal a single piece of silver.

It was Louis who had found shelter in the catacombs of Paris. The bone-filled tunnels served not only as shelter from the elements, but were an excellent place to hide from the police who were now, to the doctor 's amazement, investigating the poor girl's murder.

Louis was aware that his wife was ten years his senior. These days, he thought, she was beginning to look it. He assumed that Delphine's motive for stabbing the girl had as much to do with her color as it did with robbing her. He could tell that Delphine had taken pleasure in the kill. He knew that his wife was becoming more and more insane, and her continued ramblings about becoming famous only confirmed his suspicions. The reasons for his concern were legion. She tinkered constantly with her little blue bag and babbled in a language he'd never heard before. If he were not an atheist, he would have said she was possessed.

Finally, Delphine had crossed a line even Louis could not have imagined. She had returned to their secret corner in the catacombs with a few francs and a piece of fresh meat. When Louis saw the coins, he guessed that she had murdered another girl. That would have been trouble enough. The alarming thing was what his medical training revealed to him about the meat. Louis knew that what Delphine was cooking on the glowing coals in the fire pit was part of the victim she had robbed.

There's no doubt about it. The broken bone running through that roast is a human femur.

Delphine cut a piece of meat from the bone, stuck a fork into it, and took a bite.

"Dammit, Louis," Delphine said, still chewing on her morsel of roasted thigh, "I can't live like this. Everything was fine when we first arrived in Saint Cloud."

"Well, who would have guessed that someone from Louisiana would come there? Shit-head Methodist minister and his big mouth," said Louis.

"Some people have no mercy," said Delphine as she helped herself to another mouthful.

Dr. Lalaurie was beginning to fear Delphine himself and now decided it might be in his best interest to steal a gun as soon as the opportunity presented itself.

"I can't live like this either," Louis said. "You killed another woman, didn't you? That's what you're eating."

"Killing never bothered you in Louisiana," said Delphine.

"The slaves that had to be sacrificed for research, well, we owned them. They died so that others might live. Happens to soldiers all the time," said Louis.

"What do you know about soldiers?" Delphine scoffed. "You were never in any army."

"Well, I had my research to do," said Louis.

Louis tried to stand up, and although his recent diet had helped him shed twenty pounds, he was still obese, awkward, and out of shape.

Once he made it to his knees, he blurted out, "Enough of this. I want to go to Cuba."

He had been thinking about Cuba for some time. The climate was more to his liking. Now that Delphine had killed again, he was also concerned about the police. He doubted that they could trace the crime to her, but he knew even that would not be a concern in Cuba.

"Cuba is a horrible place," said Delphine. "No, let's go to Pau in the south. The mountain air will do us some good."

Louis made it to his feet, knocking over a stack of bones in the process. The couple left the dark madness of the Paris catacombs that night. Without any money, Louis feared it could take a year to make their way to Pau. He feared that Dr. Miller might reveal their identities to the police in Paris long before they could get to the south of France.

The choir sang the Litany of the Saints. Sheriff Dubois, Marie Laveau, and an entire fire brigade joined in singing every refrain of "*Ora pro nobis*." Philippe wore a white alb as he prostrated himself before the altar.

Just as Philippe had predicted, Father Blanc had been elevated to bishop by Pope Gregory XVI. Now, as Bishop Blanc, he was ordaining his newest priest, Reverend Father Philippe Bertrand.

Two hours later at Guy's apartment, Brigitte, Elise, and Marie were bringing turtle soup, jambalaya, bread pudding, and pecan pie from the kitchen. Guy uncorked the bottle of wine he had been saving for years, the last of three bottles he had brought from his father's vineyard in France.

Guy placed the bottle on the table and adjusted Philippe's clerical collar. "Can you believe it? My brother, a priest?" he asked.

Philippe picked up the bottle of wine, poured the first glass, and handed it to Elise.

"Philippe, I mean, Father Bertrand, I couldn't miss this occasion," said Marie. "I hear Bishop Blanc assigned you to the new parish, Saint Augustine's, is it?"

"Yes, that's right," said Philippe. "Oh, Marie, it's so good of you to be here, and Elise, you look—"

Elise interrupted. "My name is Marie now."

"Yes, I have to remember, I'm Father and you're Marie. So many changes," said Philippe.

Guy pulled a letter from his vest pocket. He and Brigitte had been planning some changes of their own. The letter in his hand confirmed their plans to move to France next year and take over the family vineyard.

"You won't believe who hasn't changed," Guy said. "I got a letter from Papa. The Lalauries turned up in France, and they are still at it. There's a reward."

"Yes, I heard Dr. Miller spotted them there, went to the police," Philippe said.

It troubled Guy that, although Delphine was no longer in New Orleans, the memory of her evil had still been able to invade even this joyous occasion.

"I hope they get the guillotine," said Brigitte.

Marie's admonition was gentle but resolute. "Brigitte, we just came from church."

"Please," said Elise, as if she could read Philippe's thoughts, "can we talk about something else? This is supposed to be a happy occasion."

"She's right," said Brigitte, picking up a ladle from the table. "I've made my special jambalaya. Let's eat. Father Bertrand, would you please bless our food?"

When he had finished, Marie Laveau thanked Philippe for his prayer and, with a mysterious smile, predicted that the prayer he would offer in the morning would be far more important.

The newspaper Delphine carried was dated 8 *Juillet* 1842 and bore a large bold headline: ÉCLIPSE SOLAIRE. Anticipation of the solar event had been the topic of discussion in every café in Pau for days. The rapid and extraordinary change from light to darkness in midafternoon no doubt felt ominous even to the most enlightened astronomers who had gathered from around Europe to study the event. To the peasants in the town of Pau, it was a portent of God's intervention; to Louis Lalaurie, a fortunate occurrence that would improve his chances of shooting a boar.

"I think the darkness will bring out the game, makes for better hunting," said Louis.

"Believe me," said Delphine, "your game is always better in the dark."

Louis carried a musket he had stolen in Paris as he walked with Delphine along a street beneath the Château de Pau toward a bridge that would lead them across the torrential Gave de Pau. Delphine's blue velvet bag had faded, but she still kept it around her neck suspended by a thin golden cord.

As the Lalauries walked across the bridge, the lunar disk concealed the entire sun, except for a faint corona. At least, that was how it appeared over France.

At the same moment in New Orleans, the sun was rising unobscured over the Mississippi. Philippe, wearing a black cassock and biretta, was pacing in front of the cathedral. His mind shifted from rehearsing parts of the Mass to his morning prayers and back to the Latin he hoped he would get right this morning. At the sound of footsteps, he squinted toward the rising sun and saw Marie and Elise approaching.

"I brought you some of my poems," said Elise, handing Philippe a stack of paper.

"*Merci*," said Philippe. He noticed that Marie had removed a small glass vial from her pocket and was opening it.

"Here," said Marie, "this will make your preaching even more…effective."

"I'm sorry, Marie," Philippe replied, trying not to sound too harsh. "I can't condone mixing your practice with this solemn…I mean, we can't equate—"

"No," agreed Marie. "Only your priesthood will reach high enough today. But a priest's first Mass is special; I want it to go well, so humor me. It's just lilac oil. It will refresh you."

At that, Marie anointed Philippe's lips with a few drops from the vial.

"Your hand is cold," said Philippe.

"Today when you pray, 'Deliver us from evil,' you will touch the edge of a very large web," said Marie.

While Philippe was entering the cathedral with Marie and Elise, Delphine and Louis were proceeding under the eclipsed sun down a dirt path, a dark forest to their right and the raging Gave de Pau on their left.

Philippe's bright green chasuble had that crisp, never-been-worn-before look, especially when compared to the ragged black cassocks and white surplices worn by the two altar boys who flanked him, left and right. Turning toward the congregation, Philippe chanted, "*Dominus vobiscum.*"

"*Et cum spiritu tuo,*" the altar servers chanted in response.

Philippe moved to the pulpit and read the gospel. The acoustics of the old cathedral were such that, from the front pew, Guy, Marie, and Elise could hear the thud as Philippe closed the book.

Philippe's voice echoed off the walls of Saint Louis Cathedral.

"As he enters the land of the Gerasenes, he is met with two who are possessed by demons, two who are so fierce that no one is safe around them. Now, it is they who ask, 'Have you come to torment us?'"

By the clock, it was seven hours later in Pau. It was at that very moment that Louis caught the first glimpse of the beast. Half a second later, the huge wild boar was charging out of the forest in front of him, snorting as it ran toward him.

The sight of its menacing tusks paralyzed Louis, preventing him from raising his musket before the boar knocked him to the ground. Blood gushed from his midsection as the animal disemboweled him with its tusks. Louis's blood pooled on the path, and a gurgling sound came from his throat. His body convulsed while the boar devoured his flesh.

Philippe's voice filled the cathedral. "The demons in these two people pleaded and cried out, 'If thou cast us out, send us into the swine.' 'Go,' he commanded them. And the demons came out and entered the swine."

On the path next to the river, Delphine stood frozen in fear. She reached up and grasped the blue velvet bag that hung from around her neck. The boar snorted, raised its head, and bolted toward her. The force of the impact knocked her unconscious before her body even hit the ground. The boar's snout dripped with blood as it began gnawing on her legs.

A gunshot rang out.

Along the tree-lined trail outside Pau, the boar reacted to being shot. It let go of Delphine's legs, squealed, and fell dead into the raging Pau River.

At the same instant that the crack of the shot muffled the gushing babble of the river, an even louder blast filled the cathedral in New Orleans. A gale-force gust of wind smashed open the doors of the church, extinguishing the candles on the altar and knocking the statue of Saint Patrick from its pedestal. The statue smashed into pieces on the white tiled floor.

Some of the congregation in New Orleans jumped to their feet when the statue hit the floor. Most of the rest turned to see what had happened. Philippe, however, continued with his sermon.

"The swine rushed into the water and perished." Philippe was shouting now. "Remember, these two demoniacs had been living in the tombs. Here is our profound hope, to be freed, not only from our demons, but also from our tombs. To obtain *l'immortalité*."

Two gendarmes, one holding a smoking pistol, approached Delphine as she writhed, moaning, in a puddle of blood.

"We have to get you to the hospital," one of them said.

The other was sniffing the air. "Rather late in the year, but do you smell lilacs?" he asked.

A plain white sheet covered Delphine as she rested on a table in a small, dark hospital room. A doctor stood next to her holding two metal clamps with wires that ran to a metal box and switch. Delphine opened her eyes.

"Ah, good, you're awake. You've been unconscious for several days," the doctor said. "You're in a hospital. I'm Dr. Lefebre."

"Dr. Lefebre?" Delphine repeated as she surfaced from delirium.

"Do you remember how you got here?" asked Lefebre.

"The boar," moaned Delphine. Recognition of the name Lefebre and a sense of abandonment and terror replaced her awareness of pain.

"You're the—"

"I had to amputate your legs, but I have attached new legs from a cadaver. It's part of my research on Galvanism," the doctor told her.

He reached under the sheet and attached the clamps to Delphine's legs, then pulled the switch on the box. Delphine screamed and convulsed on the table. A moment later, she was dead, her eyes open, fixed and dilated.

One of the same gendarmes who had brought her to the hospital ran into the room when he heard the scream. Lefebre was removing the blue velvet bag from around Delphine's neck. He put it in his pocket and covered her face with the sheet. He peeked at the clock across the room. The time was twenty minutes to twelve.

"I'm afraid she didn't make it," he told the gendarme. "Ever find out who she was?"

The gendarme looked at the paper in his hand. It was a communiqué from Paris.

"Her name was Delphine Lalaurie."

EPILOGUE

The tour guide was standing across the street from the Lalaurie mansion. The mysterious woman with the lidded basket, face still hidden by her red-and-white scarf, was at the back of the tour group. Carl, with his empty hurricane cup, stood next to his wife.

"Yes, Delphine Lalaurie," said the tour guide, "a name that will live forever. She sought immortality through fame; her husband, in science; Elise, in poetry; Philippe, through the religion of the church. Their quests for immortality intersected right here at this corner on Royal Street. Now, if you'll follow me..."

The tour group began to move. The mysterious woman decided that she would wait until the end of the tour before asking the guide about the blue velvet bag he held clutched in his hand.

"Do you believe all that?" Carl asked his wife.

The mysterious woman pulled back her red-and-white scarf and revealed her face.

It was Marie Laveau.

"I do," she said as she opened the lid to her basket. The python stuck its head out of the basket head and flicked its forked tongue.

"You do, too, don't you, Zombie?"

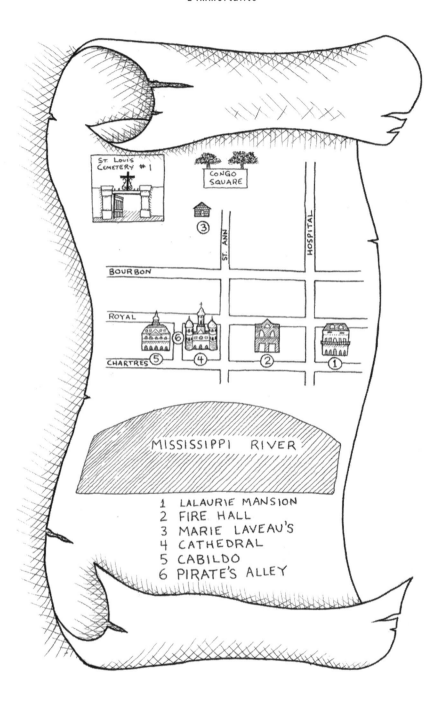

About the Author

T.R. Heinan was born in Duluth, Minnesota, and developed his love for history during his five years at Marquette University. After a brief stint as a journalist, he began a career in investment banking, specializing in the airline and motion picture industries. His retirement years have been devoted to writing and to serving orphaned and homeless children at a Mexican orphanage that he helped to establish. *L'Immortalité* is his first book-length work of historical fiction.

He is an avid traveler and was inspired to write about Delphine Lalaurie during one of his many visits to New Orleans. Heinan now resides in Tucson, Arizona, with his wife and two cats.

1140 Royal Street, the Lalaurie Mansion

Photo by T. R. Heinan

Visit us at

l-immortalite-madame-lalaurie-and-the-voodoo-queen.com